"I could do with a woman like you in my life, Fran."

She turned on him. "Too bad I'm not on offer!"

Evan continued as if he hadn't heard. "I married a woman for whom I had some feeling. We'd been close for two years, then we decided to make it legal. I wanted children. On the day of the wedding, she bolted. She waited until after the ceremony—a nice turn of the screw." His eyes narrowed on Fran's face. "I called London. My secretary read out relevant details from your personal file."

"To check whether I was suitable for your brother?" Fran hadn't forgotten how Evan had kept them apart.

"No." His bold stare swept her figure. "To see if you were suitable for me. An opportunity like this may not occur again—the chance to marry a woman who doesn't care a damn for me, nor I for her."

LILIAN PEAKE lives near the sea in England. Her first job was working for a mystery writer, employment that she says gave her an excellent insight into how an author functions. She went on to become a journalist and reported on the fashion world for a trade magazine. Later she took on an advice column, the writing of which contributed to her understanding of people's lives. Now she draws on her experiences and perception, not to mention a fertile imagination, to craft her many fine romances. She and her husband, a college principal, have three children.

Books by Lilian Peake

These books may be available at your local bookseller.

Don't miss any of our special offers. Write to us at the following address for information on our newest releases.

Harlequin Reader Service
901 Fuhrmann Blvd., P.O. Box 1397, Buffalo, NY 14240
Canadian address: P.O. Box 2800, Postal Station A,
5170 Yonge St., Willowdale, Ont. M2N 6J3

LILIAN PEAKE

ice into fire

Harlequin Books

TORONTO • NEW YORK • LONDON
AMSTERDAM • PARIS • SYDNEY • HAMBURG
STOCKHOLM • ATHENS • TOKYO • MILAN

Harlequin Presents first edition May 1986
ISBN 0-373-10886-9

Original hardcover edition published in 1985
by Mills & Boon Limited

CHAPTER ONE

'WILL you meet me there?' Ralph asked, his grey eyes on the woman across the table.

It took Fran some time to answer. The chatter of the restaurant's patrons did not intrude on her thoughts which, considering the invitation she had just received, should at least have put a curve to her lips, if not succeeding in producing a fully-fledged smile.

At last, she met the pale gaze. 'The chalet's family-owned, you said?'

'Yes, but we tell one another when we plan to go.'

'Will you tell this time, Ralph?'

It was something of a loaded question and Ralph's hesitation revealed that he recognised it as such. 'Nobody's told me they'll be using it next weekend. And it'll only be for three nights, after all.'

He had ducked the question but Fran couldn't blame him, considering the curious nature of their relationship. They went around together, they were friends—sometimes, just a little more. Now and then, they walked hand-in-hand and occasionally, even kissed.

It was a condition that Fran had imposed from the moment of their first date. No involvement, she had told him, no entanglement of the emotions. Hers were gone beyond recall, had retreated into hiding, never, she swore, to emerge again.

She had been forced to watch the slow break-up of her parents' marriage. It had been like standing on a bridge and feeling it give way beneath her feet. It would never, she vowed, happen to her.

It was simple, she had told herself. She would never

let her feelings get out of hand. She would never fall in love. Giving oneself in lovemaking was one thing, she had argued. Giving oneself body and soul into a man's keeping was another.

She wasn't going to get hurt that way. There would be no heart-searing parting from a lifelong partner; nothing like her parents' break-up for her.

Ralph had agreed to her condition, saying it was fine with him. Like her, he wanted no deep and lasting commitment. He had a career in front of him, a ready-made ladder to climb, the family's ladder. His stepfather was chairman of the family-owned publishing company—Dowd Wideworld.

Ralph's stepbrother was the corporation's chief executive. Even his mother was involved in the public relations side of the business—which, Ralph had explained at their first meeting, was how his mother and his stepfather had met.

Ralph himself worked on the sales side. He travelled a great deal, which was why the 'no involvement' part of their deal appealed to him. Fran had not specified 'no lovemaking', but that was how it had been. So far . . .

Which was why it took Fran so long to give her answer. Would she meet him at the chalet? Ralph had asked. What Ralph had not said was, Will you sleep with me there? But she would have had to be naïve indeed if she hadn't known it was in his mind.

'How will I find the chalet?' she asked, which was, she acknowledged, equal to saying—with a little more coaxing from you, I might, I just might . . .

'I'll give you directions,' he told her, his only acknowledgment of her near-capitulation registering in the slight tremor of her eyelids. 'It's about an hour's drive from Montreux. The company convention there ends midday next Friday. There's a bus that takes tourists up into the mountains for the skiing. Or I could arrange a company car——'

'Ralph, no! Thanks,' she finished more quietly, 'but it just mustn't get around your family, must it? They may think we're serious, but we're not.'

'After next weekend things will become—more than friendly between us—won't they?' he added.

His question showed that he still had doubts about whether she would say 'yes'. What's the use of refusing, she fought with herself. At twenty-four, she was no adolescent. She and Ralph had reached a point in their relationship where it was necessary for her to face facts.

Something protested inside her and she balled her fists, but she nodded. 'More than friendly.' Well, she had said it now, she had given him his answer. 'But, Ralph—no involvement, remember?'

He looked at her, his eyes giving no coherent read-out. 'Sex without love—it's not difficult for a man, you know. How a woman feels, I wouldn't know.'

Nor would I, she thought in a turmoil. His words replayed themselves—'without love, it's not difficult for a man.' The meaning hit her somewhere—not her emotions, never those, she had sworn. No, it was her pride, her femininity he had hurt. Now I'm being stupid, she reproached herself. Every time I look in the mirror, my reflection tells me . . .

What did that girl tell her? That her eyes were wide-spaced and a kind of green-grey, that her nose was neat and her mouth small—until she smiled, when it widened, giving her face an illumination like Christmas lights unexpectedly switched on.

It told her, too, that her chestnut hair, parted slightly off-centre, shone with life, that it tumbled down over her shoulders and a little beyond; that, when it was caught high in a top-knot she looked sophisticated and self-assured, as if she knew exactly where she was going in life.

I'm not 'going' anywhere, she thought, revolving her wine glass by the stem. I'm on the run, and I'll keep on running from permanency, from marriage and from love itself. Could anyone blame me? she thought. I have no parents any more, I know what an orphan feels like ... How could they do it to me?

'Fran? Have I said something?'

Before looking at him, she closed her eyes to eliminate the pain. She gave him a smile. It must have been a good effort, she thought, since he smiled back.

'A woman can——' she moistened her lips with a drink of wine, 'can enjoy the—the contact without the——' her throat needed clearing, 'the love.' I'm speaking a lie, she told herself angrily. I don't know, do I?'

'I have to go to Paris first,' she told him. He settled back in his seat, relief in every feature. 'I'm meeting the three fashion models there. The clothes I've chosen to feature in the magazine need that kind of background.'

Ralph nodded. 'I'll be at the convention. If I see you there, I'll pretend I don't know you in case the family becomes too curious about us. But,' he watched every movement the waiter made in delivering the coffee to the table, 'three days is a long time to ignore someone you——' She did not want to hear that last word, whatever it was going to be.

'You may not see me,' Fran broke in, 'not for the first day, anyway. These photo sessions can sometimes take longer than one anticipates.'

He nodded. 'We'd better make the arrangements now.' He made notes on a scrap of paper and explained them to her in detail. When he handed the paper over to her, he gave her a key. 'We all have one to the chalet. That's a spare.' He caught her hand. 'I can't wait, Fran. I like you a lot, and——'

She smiled as she tucked the paper into her bag. The skin around her mouth felt taut. 'There's no need to pretend anything, Ralph. When we meet at your family's Swiss chalet, we'll both know the score. Won't we?'

He avoided her eyes, and it worried her. But he said, 'No involvement, and that's a promise,' with an assurance that set her doubts at rest.

When Fran arrived at the Dowd Wideworld convention, the final speaker was starting his speech.

'You've left it a bit late,' a young man commented good-humouredly. 'The talking's nearly over.'

The seat beside him was the nearest to the door. Fran had slipped into it, hoping her entry into the large, ornate hall would not be noticed.

'I made it, all the same,' she answered, smiling, 'even though it's the last day.'

She had noticed the bearded young man wandering round the tower block which was the London headquarters of the Dowd publishing group. She had never spoken to him before but this was different. At a company convention like this, familiar but unidentified faces broke into smiles which demolished barriers.

The month was February, yet in the warmth of the heated conference hall, the women wore spring-weight outfits, while the men looked over-warm in their tailored suits.

'I was delayed by work,' Fran whispered. 'The fashion models I had to cope with in Paris for a photo session turned temperamental. I've just flown in from there.' She added, 'I'm fashion editor of *Woman's Choice*.'

'And I'm just a tame artist. Call what you do work?' The young man grinned and returned his attention to the speaker. Later, he said out of the side of his mouth, 'You haven't missed much. Chairman made his little speech yesterday and had to leave. Chief executive made his today and hasn't been seen since. "Important appointment," they said.' He looked at his watch and nodded towards the platform. 'Thank goodness this bloke's wad of notes is thinning out. Three days of company *bonhomie* is about as much as a thinking man can stand.'

The speaker was winding up his speech. There was general applause and the young man sighed his pleasure. 'Grub follows, drink flows,' he said.

Everyone was rising, talking and laughing. Fran gazed round the hall. The men on the platform were too far away for her to identify but there was no sign of Ralph.

The young man gestured. 'I'd take a guess by the way they're all bunching in that doorway that the food is through there. All alone?'

'It doesn't matter,' Fran started excusing herself, but her companion broke in, 'It's on the house. Come on, have a drink at least.'

Fran agreed reluctantly, adding, 'Then I must go.'

The young man said his name was Andy, and what was hers? She told him. He took her arm and urged her towards the crowded doorway. The room was large, the chandeliers were crystal and sparkled like the liquid in the glasses below. The brown velvet curtains were ceiling-to-floor and the gilt furnishings reminded Fran of the fashion houses she visited in the course of her work. Tables along two walls were stacked with food and people, holding empty plates, extended eager fingers to fill them. The post-conference release of high spirits increased to a deafening level.

'Fran,' said Andy, his voice raised to be heard,

'meet Dave, meet Mike. Mini-tycoons, all of us. We're all near the bottom of the Dowd Wideworld ladder, but we're determined to make it to the top.'

'Are we?' queried Mike, fair haired and round-faced. 'Ever found a photographer in a high managerial post? I'm not an organisation man. Didn't know you were, either, Andy.'

'I wasn't,' his friend replied, 'until I met Fran.'

There was general laughter and Fran felt herself drawn in. 'Are you new on the photographic team?' Fran asked. Mike nodded. 'No wonder I haven't seen you before. In my job, I work in conjunction with photographers.'

'You're welcome to work in conjunction with me any time, Fran,' said Mike.

Again there was laughter. The drink Andy had given her was beginning to bring the colour to Fran's cheeks. It's time, she thought, that I started to enjoy life. Time I thought about me for a change. My parents didn't ... The tingling liquid which she deliberately finished in two gulps cut off the turning inward of her thoughts and lifted her spirits to a new high. Andy gave her another drink. Dave, shorter than his friends and wearing spectacles, was saying, 'I'm not the type, either, to stand on my pals' shoulders to get above them to the top. And I'm not an artist, just a member of the circulation team, but,' he lifted his glass, smiling, 'if I'd met Fran first, who knows how far up the careers ladder I might have pushed myself?'

'I didn't realise,' Fran put in, feeling herself growing more animated than for a long time, 'that "Ambitious Man" was such a dying species.'

Andy, on his fourth drink, swayed nearer. Mike pressed his drinking arm against hers and Dave took a small but definite step towards her. 'You're something of that yourself,' commented Andy, his words swaying a little, too. 'You've got rarity value. Beautiful, got the lot——'

'Right shape,' Mike inserted, pretending to hold a camera to his eye.

'And intelligent,' Dave added, moving his spectacles partway down his nose, 'also, touch-me-not.' He pushed them back.

Fran started at his perceptive comment, began to say, 'How did you——?' when a voice asked, 'Miss Williams? Miss Francesca Williams?'

Fran swung round. A woman she had never seen before was standing beside her. She was smiling in a friendly, yet impersonal way. 'You were pointed out to me as the girl in the outfit that matched her hair.' Fran looked down quickly. She hadn't even realised that it did.

'Sorry I startled you,' the woman said, 'I'm Carole Huntley. I've been asked to give this to you.' She held out a letter. The envelope bore no name, the flap was sealed.

Fran accepted it with a murmured thanks and a quick, uncertain smile. The woman disappeared into the crowd. She had not explained her identity, nor had she revealed who had given her the letter to pass on.

'Go on, open it,' she heard Mike say. 'Secret assignation?' Dave joked. 'Sudden promotion as a result of arriving late for the Dowd Wideworld Corporation convention?' Andy added.

'Must be,' Dave commented, 'since the chairman's secretary gave it to you.'

Fran caught her breath. 'Chairman's secretary?' Had Ralph told the family about her, after all? Was their meeting at the chalet no longer possible? 'I—er— didn't know who Miss Huntley was,' she remarked, to cover the fact that the woman's identity had shaken her.

The note said, 'Fran: Sorry, unable to make it tonight. Unexpectedly called back to London. Go to chalet as arranged. You'll find necessary supplies laid on. Will join you Saturday afternoon. Ralph.'

'Good news?' asked Andy. All three had been watching her.

'Why do you ask that?' Fran slid the note back into the envelope.

'You seemed to cheer up as you read it.'

Mike nodded. 'You almost smiled.'

'I didn't.' She frowned. 'Did I?' Had she smiled, she wondered. She couldn't deny that there had been more relief than disappointment in her secret reaction. But why relief? She knew the answer at once—that night she would be sleeping alone, after all.

It was dark when Fran arrived. There had been lights on the way, shining out from rectangular windows, glistening on the snow's crust. The engine of the bus, which was full of tourists, had moaned at the gradients. Now and then, Fran swallowed to clear her ears of a curious deafness, probably the result of increasing altitude.

Before leaving, she had found a powder room where she had been able to change out of her neat suit and blouse and pull on warm slacks, sweater and thick jacket. At Ralph's suggestion she had bought herself some strong shoes and thick-lined boots, the warmth of which she appreciated as the bus had climbed higher.

In the town centre, the bus halted. Colour flashed everywhere, piercing the darkness. Some shops advertised souvenirs, others ski hire. Cafés and restaurants were filled to the doors. Fran stepped down from the coach feeling bewildered. Was the chalet here, she wondered.

The driver told her in good English that it was a climb, somewhere up there—he indicated a collection of wooden buildings, dark shapes topped with wide white roofs. A member of a group broke away and smiled at Fran.

'We're going up there,' she said. 'Like to join us?'

Fran did so gladly, and they told her they thought they knew the chalet she wanted. 'Whenever we've come,' the young woman said, 'there's been someone at that place.'

One of the group took her across, using his torch. 'Come for a week's skiing, like us?' he asked.

Fran shook her head. 'Just the weekend.'

'Well,' he turned away with a smile, 'you certainly won't learn to ski in that time. Unless you know already?' Fran shook her head, thanking him. He lifted his hand, his torch light moving away. 'Enjoy your short break,' he called, adding with laughter, 'Don't attempt too many ski jumps!'

The chalet windows were shuttered, giving the place a closed-in look, as if it were saying 'go away, stranger.' Yet, when the key turned and the door swung open, the warmth reached out. It hadn't been necessary to see the wall radiators to know that the place was centrally-heated.

And occupied, surely? Finding the light switch, Fran looked around her. Everywhere there was wood, shining and varnished, the knots in it speckling the walls with a darker brown.

The floor was hard, probably of stone, but covered in serviceable green carpeting. There were doors leading off the long entrance corridor and Fran found herself in a good-sized kitchen containing the best of modern equipment. Leading out from there, was a spacious lounge and dining room combined.

The furniture here was wooden too, and varnished to

match the walls. The curtains, which had been drawn across to cover the windows, were a burnt-orange patterned material, and this was echoed in the upholstery and the cloth which had been spread across the dining table. On the walls were pictures, posters of mountains and snow scenes. There were even two or three pot plants on artistically fixed shelves.

The plants looked freshly-watered. The whole atmosphere was charged with a lived-in feeling. Had Ralph been able to come? Had the note been simply a precautionary measure, just in case she had been disappointed by his possible non-appearance? Disappointed? she asked herself, putting down her suitcase. Is that what she would have been?

Her tired mind dodged the answer and she returned to the kitchen, looking for food. There were packet mixes in the cupboard, food in the fridge for heating through. There were two or three cartons of milk, also, one of which had been opened. Its smell was fresh, the 'sell-by' date reassuring.

There had to be someone in occupation! Putting everything down, she hurried along the hall to the wooden staircase, passing the open door of the shower-room on the way. Her voice calling 'Ralph?' was carried around the large, shadowy building. There was no reply.

Her feet took her swiftly up the stairs. Switching on lights, she counted four large bedrooms. One of them was scattered with belongings, the thick quilt thrown across the double bed on to which clothes had been dropped. One thing was obvious—whoever had been living in the chalet was not there now. And whoever it was, was as untidy in his ways as he was careless in his abandonment of half-used food. Yet, Fran reasoned, pushing at her hair, that milk was still fresh.

Hunger gnawed. After a hurried glance into the

other bedrooms, all of which were in an immaculate state, Fran ran down to satisfy her appetite. Later, taking her coffee into the living-room, she sank into a low, cushioned chair. It had been a long day. Her hunger might have been assuaged, but her limbs and her spirits were still weary.

Placing her empty cup on the table, she went across to the transistor radio that stood on the sideboard. Searching for music, preferably of the soothing kind, she returned to the chair and curled her legs under her.

The softly melodic sound pacified her underlying anxieties. Only as she closed her eyes and relaxed did she realise she had any worries.

If I let myself think about why I'm here, she mused, I'll start to wonder—should I have come? Tonight, at least, she reassured herself, with Ralph far away, I'll have no cause for regret. She darted after the thought. Regret was an emotion, and her arrangement with Ralph had been on the basis of no such complication.

She stirred restlessly. It had to be so. She must remain true to herself, she would go through life emotionally independent, relying on no one else for her happiness.

Thirty years, she reasoned with herself for the hundredth time, you'd have thought, wouldn't you, that Mother and Dad would have managed to make their thirty-year marriage last? All right, so they'd married at not quite twenty, but they'd been together long enough, hadn't they, to have learned how to overcome their differences?

We've grown apart, darling, her mother had said, that day she had broken the news of the impending separation. Grown *apart*? Fran had asked unbelievingly. Over thirty years, Fran had argued, there's surely only one way to grow and that was together, wasn't it? Darling, her mother had replied, the trouble is—all right, so we married young—we've never grown *up*. How can I make you understand?

Never, Fran had answered, never in a million years! You loved each other, didn't you? You must have, to have had me. Tears rose yet again as Fran recalled her mother's slow shake of the head. Warm motherly arms had come round her. 'You're still a babe yourself,' her mother had said. 'One day, when you've got a man of your own, you'll understand.' Her mother's tears had been damp on Fran's cheeks as she had walked away.

Man of my own? Fran thought, folding her arms across her middle and settling more deeply into the chair. Never, she vowed, never ... The warmth seeped into her, the music drowned out the past.

There was a stirring of air, like a breeze fanning her face; a movement that disturbed through its very quietness. Ralph? She heard the name in her head. Who else could it be? Her eyes came open and she found that her hands were gripping the chair's arms. There was no music now. The radio had been switched off.

The two eyes into which she stared were not pale grey as she had expected. They were, instead, blue and hard and slightly narrowed as though their owner's thoughts were hard, too, and mistrustful. The rest of him was solid and broad and tall, with black hair untidy from wind riffling through it.

He wore a scarlet and yellow anorak and close fitting dark ski pants. He put down the gloves and goggles he was holding and proceeded to unzip his jacket, staring at her all the time.

'Who——?' Fran struggled for breath which she seemed to have been holding for ever. Her stiffly curled legs found the floor, her gripping hands pulled her upright. Her fingers strayed over the back of her hair which seemed to have straggled free from the top-knot into which she had twisted it that morning in Paris. She pulled her sweater into place and tried again. 'Who——?'

'Are *you*?' The stranger took up her question, tossing it back to her. He pulled free of the jacket. The eyes, Fran noticed, were smiling now and very blue. How could I ever have thought, she asked herself, that they were suspicious and hostile?

'I'm Fran, Fran Williams, a friend of——' She couldn't tell him! He might be one of the family. The last thing Ralph would want her to do was to let their friendship be known to the Dowds. 'Who *are* you?' she asked, tacking on a smile because it was imperative now that she had an answer.

'A friend of——' laughter lit his eyes as he imitated her hesitation, 'the family.'

'A friend? Oh!'

'Why the sigh? Was it relief? Did you suspect I was a member of the Dowd clan? I'm Johnny Black.'

She frowned. 'Ralph's never mentioned——' She had said his name!

'You're a friend of his.'

He had spoken the words with such confidence, she grew anxious. 'How do you know?'

'You told me.' The blue eyes were still smiling. 'But you did. When you woke up just now you said his name.'

So it hadn't just been in her head? How could she have let Ralph down so? 'A friend,' she conceded, her smile tight, 'we met at work.'

'Were you expecting him?' What else could she do, she argued with herself, but nod? 'And I came instead. You must be disappointed.'

'Disappointed?' She frowned at the note of surprise in her voice. 'Yes, yes, I am. Very disappointed.'

'You mean, he let you down without a word? Brought you here looking forward to a lovers' meeting, then didn't bother to come?'

He was leaning back against the table, hands in pockets. If he hadn't sounded so solicitous on her behalf, so sorry for the situation in which he assumed she had unexpectedly found herself, her anxieties at his questioning would have been revived.

His relaxed manner encouraged her to let down her guard. But only by an inch, she told herself. 'He isn't coming until tomorrow. He sent me a note. The chairman's sec——' Nervous fingers tugged at her sweater's neckline. Had it passed him by, those giveaway words? 'Do you—do you work for Dowd's?'

'As a matter of fact, I do.' He had either missed her near-disastrous error or regarded it as of no consequence. He wandered round the large room, felt the temperature of the radiators, moved to twitch a drawn curtain into place. 'Nothing exciting. In admin. You?'

Fran nodded, resuming her seat. 'Fashion editor of *Woman's Choice*.'

He returned to stand in front of her, looking down. 'Well, well. Face to face with a journalist. Something I vowed I'd never do.'

'Why, are you an important person?'

His head went back in laughter, his strong throat moving. 'A celebrity, no less,' he mocked. 'Like to interview me? Desk-bound administrator, amateur skier, unattached roamer of the world. Hobbies— reading, music—appreciation of.'

She took up his faintly satirical manner. 'You'd rate your greatest achievement as being so friendly with the Dowd family, they've even given you a key to this chalet so that you can come and go as you please?' She put her head on one side, watching him.

Had she caught him on a tender spot? Surely she had not imagined that dash of irritation across his eyes?

'A journalist's trick question, is it? You're implying I should add "social climber" to my list of hobbies?' The smile was back, the eyes a warm blue. 'Is that what you think I am?' He folded his arms, looking into her upturned face. 'If so, what does that make you, Miss Williams?'

'Please call me Fran.' She was frowning. The question worried her, the man's puzzling character still more. 'I'm Ralph's friend, that's all.'

'Friends as well as lovers? That's some relationship.'

'Not lovers, Mr Black,' she replied, putting an edge to her tone.

'Call me Johnny,' was the speedy return. 'No, Fran?' He seemed genuinely surprised. 'When he comes, what'll you do—sleep in separate bedrooms? I grant you there are plenty to choose from. But you surely can't expect me to believe Ralph got you to come all the way here so that he could act the perfect gentleman and watch you shut the bedroom door in his face?'

'I'm not asking you to believe anything,' Fran answered with spirit. 'If he—we had intended to make love, our visit wouldn't have coincided with yours, would it?'

'He didn't know I was coming.' His tone said 'beat that'.

Fran silently admitted it was a trump card—almost. 'He told me,' she pointed out, 'that the family let each other know when they intend coming here.' The raised eyebrows above the intensely blue eyes jogged her mind. 'All right, so you're a family friend. I assumed that his statement covered friends as well as relatives.'

The broad shoulders lifted and fell, their owner turned away. 'So I've spoilt your secret weekend of lovemaking.'

'We were not going to make love!'

He turned back. 'So what were you going to make—sex?'

Fran coloured deeply at the distaste in his tone. 'You're just a family friend, you said. So why are you so concerned about Ralph's private life?'

'I notice you didn't answer my question.'

'Any more than you've answered mine.' Fran glared into his eyes.

There was a dangerous silence, as if a mine field separated them. The taut mouth curved, its owner exploding into laughter. Fran put fingertips to her forehead, feeling the moisture. How had he managed to get her into such a state of tension? He was a passing stranger. He would probably be moving out tomorrow.

His hand moved towards her. 'Truce, friend?' he suggested, his dark eyebrows arching.

With a curious sense of relief, Fran nodded and put her hand in his. He held it, turning it over to examine the palm. 'Heartline?' he asked, his finger tracing the line. Then his brows drew together with simulated disbelief. 'Is there one?'

She retrieved her hand quickly, wondering why the touch of his finger made her hand tingle. 'Only in the physical sense,' she told him. 'It works perfectly well as the pump it's supposed to be.'

His fingers spread out over his hips. 'Your exterior is so enticing, Francesca——'

Fran started. When had she told him her full name?

'—it triggers my reach-out-and-get-her reflexes. Yet you're trying to tell me you're a heartless woman? I don't believe you.' His head was back, his eyes assessed her from partly lowered lids.

'If by heartless you mean is there a place in my life for love,' she parried, 'the answer's no.'

'So there's going to be no man in your life?'

Fran's brows pleated with annoyance, then she sorted through her smiles and found a bright one. 'I only met you half-an-hour ago, so I don't see why I should answer that question, do you?'

Her attempt to put the man in his place did not succeed. 'What about Ralph?' he probed.

'There's no need to worry about Ralph,' she said easily. 'He's known my feelings on the subject from the first time we went together. No emotional involvement.'

He moved nearer, and his eyes did a swift survey of her shape. 'What terrible thing happened to cause you to make such a condition?'

'It didn't happen to me. It was my——' She couldn't speak about such a private matter to a stranger. 'I'd rather not talk about it, if you don't mind,' she added, looking down to avoid the penetrating gaze.

'Suppose I said I do mind?' The question was asked softly, bringing her head up. 'That I'd like to know for—shall we say—personal reasons?'

'I don't understand,' she answered, her hazel eyes frowning into the blue ones above her.

'That I'd like to know,' he went on as if she had not spoken, 'if the field is clear. Because the prospect,' he put his foot on the corner of the chair in which she sat and rested his arm on his knee, 'of a night or two shared with a beautiful woman who's more than willing to come to a man with no fuss afterwards about a loving relationship is too good to miss.'

She looked at him and saw his narrowed glance. The world tilted and swung around and she realised that, despite her determination to keep her emotional temperature low, his masculinity was having a frightening impact on her senses. She made to rise, but found herself imprisoned by the inner thigh he had placed next to her. The arm of the chair formed the other barrier. She was locked in.

'Please,' she said, 'will you let me stand up? I'm tired. I'd like to go to bed.'

'Exactly,' he said, his tone still soft and enticing.

Her heart began to pound. Who was this man? Why hadn't she been told he might come? Worse, had he really any right to be in the place? She pushed at the thigh and discovered its iron hardness. Something in her, more potent than fear, responded to the feel of the man, and that really scared her.

Taking his time, he removed his foot and moved back a pace. Fran immediately stood up and tensed for running. He blocked her path and held her arms.

'Will you let me go?' she asked, her voice barely a whisper.

He must have seen her fear since he released her, standing aside.

'Have you chosen a room?'

The question reached her as she arrived at her pile of belongings near the door. Bending to pick them up, she answered without turning, 'Not yet. Does it matter which one?'

'You can use any of the three remaining rooms.'

Fran nodded, then felt the suitcase taken from her fingers. 'I can manage, thanks,' she tried to protest, but firm fingers directed her towards the stairs.

The room he took her to was opposite the one she had seen earlier with belongings scattered around. It was large and designed for function more than comfort. There were two beds and furniture in matching wood, and a scattering of colourful rugs over the wooden floor.

'This is fine.' She turned to him with a smile and found his eyes on her.

He nodded, giving away none of his thoughts. 'You've found the bathroom? Good. If you want anything—any time—I'm across there. Okay?'

'Thanks again.' She watched him go and discovered the tension in her clasped hands. She flexed her fingers quickly, and told herself over and over, No man is going to get under my guard—least of all a tall, good-looking man who's almost certainly got an address book full of women's names.

As she extracted the items she would need from her suitcase, she wondered exactly what Ralph had in mind. Each bedroom seemed to have two beds. Then she told herself not to be so foolish as to believe that Ralph intended anything other than sharing hers.

Something in her shrank a little at the idea. It was the cold-bloodedness, she told herself, then followed it up with the silent admonishment that that was what she wanted, wasn't it, or ever would want from a man? And who better than with a sensitive, quiet person like Ralph? She liked him, she liked him a lot. Wasn't that enough?

Morning came swiftly after a surprisingly sweet night's rest. Fran flung back the bed cover, wanting to run to the window—only to remember that its shutters were closed. The inner windows opened wide as she pulled them, but the shutters would not give.

With her fist she hammered, only to stand back defeated. She lifted her hand to try again and heard a sound behind her. Arm still upraised, she turned to find the man called Johnny coming across the room.

'Trouble?' he asked, looking down at her and smiling. He wore a thigh-length towelling robe tied at the waist. Under it there seemed to be nothing. His eyes, as they moved over her, held not amusement but a very male look.

So why, she asked herself, shouldn't her heart speed up? She was only human. A very female reaction was taking place inside her, that was all, the desire in her responding, nothing else. A woman could react to a man, couldn't she, without any trace of emotion?

He reached out and lowered her arm. 'That's better,' he said, his lips curving widely. 'Feminine aggression is something I can do without first thing in the morning—unless it's in the right place.' His skating eyes told her exactly where he meant. 'Having trouble?' He dealt with the lock, showing her how, then threw the shutters wide.

The view that was revealed drew from her a gasping breath. She looked with wonder at the startling white of the encircling mountains and saw that, here and there, the snow blanket was probed by rocky ridges, and speckled with green as a forest of conifers, draped in white, climbed upwards.

'It's fantastic,' she exclaimed, then a shiver caught her and she realised how little of her body was covered by her short nightdress.

Two arms came round her, drawing her back against a hard male body. 'Share my warmth,' the low deep voice invited, curling around her ear.

Fran jerked, trying to free herself. 'I'm not cold,' she denied, then to her annoyance she shivered again. This time it was not a blast of icy air that caused it. It was her acute awareness of the man whose arms were locked around her waist. Her dismay at the effect his closeness was having made her pull at his clasped hands.

To her surprise, they gave, only to settle on her shoulders. She gathered her strength for another pull away from him, but found herself pinioned by the stroking feel of the hands that were running the length of her bare arms.

When all the nerves in her body did a mad dance under the impact of lips seeking the soft sensitivity of her neck, she jerked violently away. 'What are you doing?' she demanded, swinging round and facing her tormentor. 'I hardly know you, yet you think I'd——'

'Wouldn't you?' The blue eyes mocked. 'If you knew me just a little longer—say tonight—would you?'

'I wouldn't, I——' Again, she looked down at herself, realising just how much of her his straying eyes were seeing. The pouting hardening of her breasts, for instance, under the impact of his magnetism ... It was someone else in her that, unresisting, watched him close the gap between them.

His arms around her were purposeful but held no force as he pulled her to him. Or had she gone there of her own accord? All thought was blotted out by the placing of his mouth over hers, by the caressing of his palms over her back and hips, by the gentle easing of himself against her.

This is wrong! The warning came from a small but insistent voice in her mind. How could it be wrong, she answered back, when the man her arms had crept around was as attractive as this man was?

If it were Ralph doing this to me, she thought, I'd be allowing him to go on without a thought of reproach. But Ralph would never in a hundred years do this to me ... Her brain was fighting with her clamouring responses—and losing out.

His hand was at the back of her head, holding it still for his lips to continue their lingering exploration of hers. His other hand had moved to find her breasts' fullness and she gasped at its audacity and the shattering effect it was having on her feelings.

She made a determined attempt to free herself by

pushing at his arms. To her surprise, they parted, letting her go. His hands slipped into his robe pockets and his faintly ironic smile matched the diamond glitter in his eyes.

'If that's how you respond without any kind of involvement,' his voice was husky. 'how would you respond with it?'

'You'll never know.' She wrapped her arms around her chilled body. 'Nor will I. It's simply not going to happen to me. I told you last night, didn't I?'

'You told me about the limits you've put on your affair with Ralph. Poor Ralph.'

'Don't pity Ralph. He's accepted the condition. And we're not having an affair. There's been nothing really serious between us so far, but this weekend we——'

'You were going to remedy that?' He had smiled as he had spoken, making the words into a question, not a criticism. All the same, Fran felt anger rise. He had manoeuvred her into being indiscreet.

'What if we were?' she challenged. 'It's our business how far we allow our friendship to develop. Ralph understands the situation completely and accepts it. He's no more in love with me than I am with him.'

The man called Johnny nodded, but Fran did not get the impression that he understood. I suppose, she reasoned, that isn't surprising, since I haven't told him my reasons for deciding I'd never let myself love a man enough to want to marry him. But I'm not telling him, she vowed.

'Can you ski?' He had changed the subject and Fran felt relief untense her muscles.

She shook her head. 'You?'

'I'm no expert but I enjoy what I can do. Out there,' he gestured to the mountains beyond the window, 'there are nursery slopes for beginners. Like to have a try?'

Fran came alive with anticipation. 'Very much.'
Again, she looked down at herself, then looked up.
The colour was in her cheeks again at the return of his
look of male desire. He had followed her eyes.

'We can get you kitted out, if that's all that's
worrying you. There's a hire shop in the town.'

'When—what time shall we go? I must get dressed.'

'I was wondering when that would occur to you.
Maybe you don't realise how provocative you are in
next to nothing?' She could not fault his smile, but
there was disbelief in his tone.

She answered with a smile of her own, but her
words warned. 'I'm not any man's, Johnny.'

It seemed he had not heard the warning, since he
took a step towards her. 'You aren't? Last night you
nearly had me fooled, not to mention this morning. If
you hadn't been so tired at bedtime, I'd have proved
by the time you'd made it to bed that what you're
saying now is wrong. Come to that,' his muscled body
came to a stop in front of her, 'there's no time like
now.'

His arms came out slowly and Fran felt herself
transfixed. Move, she shouted silently at herself, get
out of his reach. For heaven's sake, use your instinct
for self-preservation. This man could undo all your
promises to yourself ... he's got the pulling power,
the knowledge ... *and tremendous attraction.*

When his hands settled on her arms, she let out a
cry of 'No!' as if his touch had burnt her. She found
herself at the door, pulling it wide and standing aside.
'Please go.'

He complied, but with mockery in his eyes.

CHAPTER TWO

'ARE you wearing sun cream?' Johnny Black asked.

Fran nodded. 'You insisted that I should buy some, so I thought I might as well use it, but it's so cold out there, I couldn't imagine why.'

'I'll tell you. The temperature in the shade might be around zero, but in the sun it can be several degrees above. It feels very warm to the skin and after a while, it starts to burn.' He ran a finger down her cheek. 'And it would be a pity if a pretty face like yours had to be covered with a protective mask.'

Fran moved her head to dislodge the finger. If only he wouldn't keep touching her . . . 'I feel overdressed,' she said, looking down at the ski clothes she had bought. Johnny had gone into the shop with her and given advice and sometimes, instructions.

'When you get out there, you'll be glad of those extra layers. Also, they'll help to buffer you when you fall.' He smiled at her look of alarm. 'We all have to be prepared to fall sometimes. Especially beginners. You might get a few grazes. Still willing to come?'

'Why do you think I'm wearing this outfit? I realised I might fall over. I'm taking a calculated risk.'

'Hard-headed little puss, aren't you?' Had her imagination put a hard gleam into his eye? His smile put up her rate of heartbeats. 'Follow me, calculating woman.'

They collected their skis from a large ground floor room which was there, Johnny explained, for the storage of dripping skis and wet ski clothes. In a corner, a central heating boiler was tucked away.

Walking slowly down to the town, Fran learned how to shoulder her skis and ski sticks. 'You'll find them heavy,' her companion warned.

'I don't mind,' she remarked, laughing up at him. 'I won't ask you to carry them for me.'

'Ask away,' he answered laconically, 'I wouldn't even if you did.'

Fran shook her head, too excited to take offence at his bluntness. The jig-saw pieces that made up the atmosphere—the tall, self-possessed, bronzed men and women all around and with whom her companion fitted in so well; the tingling cold which bit at any piece of exposed skin; the impact of the sun's unexpected warmth—were joining together to lift her to a level of happiness she had not experienced since childhood.

He showed her how to walk in ski boots and, after arriving at the beginners' slopes, how to fix skis to the boots. He taught her how to balance, how to side-step upwards, and how to ski down a few feet, his arm comfortably round her.

It was impossible not to lose her balance, Fran discovered, but most of the falls she was ready for. 'You'll have some bruises,' Johnny warned, watching her indulgently, laughing now and then.

She had turned to listen and lost her balance, falling backwards. He was there in a moment, arm extended, breaking her fall and going down with her.

Laughing, they stayed together in a heap lying on their sides, their skis entangled. Her face was scarlet with cold and sun combined, and with an intense enjoyment of the exercise. He sobered as their eyes became as enmeshed as their skis, and Fran felt her heart leap like a skier taking a jump. The laughter stilled on her lips as she saw his face at close quarters. An impulse brought her fingertips into contact with his cleanshaven cheeks, the strong chin, the quirking smile playing over his mouth.

When she lifted her eyes and saw the faint flicker of his eyelids, there was a tug inside her. She realised in one swift moment that, in this stranger's company, her resolution to keep her emotional distance was in danger of being forgotten. Her exploring hand lifted, losing contact with his face, and hovered uncertainly.

Strong male fingers seized it. 'Thanks,' Johnny Black addressed it, 'for breaking through her barriers.' He put the palm to his lips and held her eyes with his, but he talked again to her hand. 'Go back and tell her she's as warm-blooded as the rest of us.'

Fran snatched her hand away. 'Will you let me get up!' she exclaimed, annoyance making her frown. 'It's damp down here. And I want to ski some more.'

'There's a price for release.' His eyes danced. 'I want the lips of the owner of that hand. Otherwise, we stay down here all day.' Someone skied past. 'Despite the danger of being cut to pieces by the rest of the stumbling beginners.'

She tried to rise, but he stopped her. 'Our immediate futures are inextricably entwined,' he averred. 'You can't release your skis from mine without my help. You'll have to pay that price.' He pulled her towards him, finding the back of her neck beneath the pull-on hat she was wearing. He guided her head towards him and pressed it back into his hand with the pressure of his mouth.

'Please,' she gasped as he drew away, 'now help me up.'

He lifted himself on to his elbow and looked down at her. 'Was the price so terrible? Now be truthful.'

She shook her head and whispered 'no', then closed her eyes on his broad, self-congratulatory smile.

'Put your gloves back on,' he advised, when they

were standing again. 'Now show me how much you've learned.'

Wanting to please him, Fran walked awkwardly up the slope, then very carefully manoeuvred herself round to face him some distance away. With her ski sticks she found her balance, then pushed herself forward. Her feet kept going of their own momentum and she lost her confidence.

'Johnny!' she cried, swaying from side to side.

'Hold on,' he shouted, 'keep upright, keep going.'

'Help me!' she cried and her skis carried her, her arms raised, holding the sticks aloft, her balance perilously close to being lost.

Strong arms outstretched were her goal and she dropped the sticks as she shot into them. They closed around her and she laughed and cried like a child, her fear turning into triumph as she said, 'I kept going, I didn't fall!'

Her arms went round the warmly padded waist and body that supported her, and her cheek rested on the shoulder that jerked beneath her with laughter. Her elation merged with his good humour and when his mouth rooted for a bare patch of neck beneath the upturned collar of her jacket, she did not pull away.

The sensation of moving lips against the skin beneath her ear sent more shivers down her back than any impact of snow or ice she had felt that morning. 'Don't, Johnny,' she managed through chattering teeth, 'please don't.' All she heard in answer was a low chuckle followed by the sting of a nipped earlobe.

He held her away then, and she tipped back her head to look at him, finding in his features a warming familiarity as though he had been her friend for years. Friend? she asked herself. Was it really friendship she wanted from this man, or . . .?

Nothing, she thought angrily, I want nothing from

him. Ralph's my friend, and tonight, who knows, maybe more than friend? He was arriving that afternoon. The fact should have pleased her, since that was why she was there, wasn't it, she nudged her sense of loyalty.

Johnny looked at his watch. 'Time to go. The lifts and cable cars stop at midday. They start again for a couple of hours at two o'clock. Game for another beginner's class?'

Fran's heart took a dive, then righted itself. The skiing session had been two hours of pure delight, a morning out of time, unexpected and never to be repeated. The man in whose company she had found so much enjoyment would probably be on his way by evening.

'Ralph's coming. Thanks, all the same. But don't let that stop you from skiing.'

'Oh, it won't,' he said with mock-seriousness. 'It'll get me out of the way, won't it, while you spend a couple of hours in Ralph's arms.'

Fran flushed and was glad her face was partly hidden by her upturned jacket collar. As they walked, he looked at her. Was he waiting for a denial? She did not give him one. Instead, she provoked, 'When are you leaving the chalet?'

He had bent down to collect his skis, so she could not see his expression as he replied, 'You really do want me out of the way, don't you?'

'I don't know what I want.' Her answer came spontaneously, surprising even her.

Johnny Black looked up quickly, eyebrow quirked. It brought the colour rushing back to Fran's cheeks. He said, hoisting the skis on to his shoulder, 'That wasn't the impression you gave me back there. You knew exactly where you wanted to be—in my arms.'

Her high colour persisted, but her bright eyes

opposed him. 'It was part of the fun,' she declared, 'like—like the spur-of-the-moment expression of pleasure that children give.'

'The woman I had in my arms back there,' he said, 'was no child, believe me.' His eyelids were half-closed as he looked at her, his long, dark lashes throwing shadows on to his cheeks. Fran found herself studying them, then dived to pick up her skis to keep her hands occupied before her fingers went their own way again and reached out to touch him.

After a refreshing meal of varied cheeses and chunky bread with a mixed salad which Johnny prepared with surprising expertise, Fran found herself alone.

Johnny had taken his leave with a mocking, 'I'll stay out an hour or so longer than usual. Let me give you a bit of advice, Francesca.' She jumped again at his use of her full name. Had he caught a glimpse of her passport while she had slept in the armchair? Had he, perhaps, taken it from her handbag to check on her identity? After all, he had not expected her to be there any more than she had expected to see him.

'When your boyfriend comes,' he was saying, 'put some welcoming warmth into that efficient pump of yours which you call your heart. Let a man at least think you have some feeling for him, otherwise you might find him reaching for his wallet in the belief that he's with a woman who expects payment.'

'I don't want your advice, thank you,' Fran had called after him, then slammed the door. Besides putting the heat back into her cheeks, his words had left their mark. She smarted under their impact, but told herself that her welcome to Ralph would be warm. Anyway, hadn't he also said he was not ready for a deep relationship?

Her thoughts tripped over themselves. What was

she doing, trying to justify her actions, silently if not aloud, to a man who was not even a member of Ralph's family?

Fran found that the hours of the afternoon passed slowly. She had washed her hair, drying it with a towel. The clothes she had changed into were comfortable yet stylish, the colour patterns on the knitted top brightening up the darkening day. She stood at the window playing with the chunky beads round her neck and watching the whiteness of the mountains deepen into grey shadows, then come alive with brightly-dressed people returning from the slopes.

Any moment, she estimated, Johnny would come in. He would, she knew, joke about Ralph's absence, saying probably that she had frozen him out, after all, with her coldness.

When he did return, he went first to the ski room. Fran heard the clatter of his skiing equipment interspersed with his raised voice singing a few words of a bawdy song.

The irony of the words was in his smile as he entered the main living room where Fran lingered near the telephone. 'Was I out long enough?' he asked.

'He hasn't come,' she said flatly. 'He said he'd be here this afternoon.' She consulted her watch for the fiftieth time. 'Is six o'clock still afternoon?'

He made a doubtful face and shook his head. 'Early evening. He's late. Maybe he couldn't face your lukewarm welcome. Maybe the thought of a passive, lifeless sleeping partner lying beside him in the small hours of the night made him cancel his flight.'

'You're wrong.' He had put her on the defensive and it touched her temper. 'He knew when we arranged this meeting how it would be between us.'

'All give on his part and all take on yours?'

'You keep trying to put me in the wrong,' she accused. 'I don't understand why you're so concerned about Ralph Sadler. He's——'

The 'phone rang and she dived to silence it. 'Yes? Ralph?' She listened, frowning 'You're not coming? Going to Frankfurt for a conference? You'll be staying in your stepbrother's apartment a few miles away? No, I couldn't possibly join you, Ralph. You were supposed to come here. It's why I came, isn't it?'

If there were tears in her voice, it was because of the awkward situation he had plunged her into, and which was becoming impossible to handle, like the person called Johnny Black.

Fran put her back to the man who hovered in the doorway. She was certain he was smiling, and it wouldn't be with kindly commiseration.

'It was very short notice, wasn't it? Have you got to go? You couldn't come just for tomorrow?' Now why had she asked that question? She knew the answer at once—to form a barrier between herself and the man over there who was standing so quietly, like a predator about to pounce. She sensed the smile had gone.

'Who's sent you away so suddenly? It was your stepbrother? Ralph, I'm not alone. A friend of the family's staying here.' There was a long silence from the other end. 'His name,' she went on, 'is Johnny, Johnny Black. Do you know him? Tall, dark haired. He's been teaching me how to——' Ralph made a sound and Fran asked urgently, 'What did you say?' Her eyes came round slowly to rest on the man leaning back against the door. His arms were folded, his legs crossed at the ankles.

Fran's heart started hammering. 'He's who? I can't hear you clearly. Ralph, he's a family friend. He told me. He——'

'Give it to me.' The 'phone was removed from her

grasp, the command given tersely. It was as though the man called Johnny Black had undergone a personality change. 'Ralph?' he rapped out. 'You're still in London? You've a plane to catch. You're cutting it fine.' He listened, turning his back on Fran as she had done to him. 'Okay, okay,' he said, like a parent soothing a child. 'It's tough luck she doesn't reciprocate. I know how it feels. Like being kicked in the——' he looked round, turned back, 'teeth.' He listened again. 'Yes,' came the dry comment, 'I'll tell her how much you love her.' The receiver clattered down.

'Who are you?'

The man turned slowly to face the wide, apprehensive eyes. 'I'm Ralph's stepbrother.' He smiled without amusement. 'Will I do in his place?'

A curious fear dried Fran's mouth. 'You mean you're Evan Dowd?' He inclined his head. 'Your name isn't really Johnny Black?'

She didn't want him to shake his head, agreeing that it wasn't. There had been something very special about Johnny Black. She didn't want to let him go out of existence.

'Evan is the Welsh form of John,' he explained. 'Dowd comes a little vaguely from the Irish for black.'

'You must have used that name many times before,' she accused. 'Probably when checking on Ralph's other girlfriends. No wonder Ralph seemed so upset when I told him your false name.'

Fran paused, eyes full of accusation. 'So it was you,' the idea had come to her suddenly, 'who gave the chairman's secretary that note to pass to me.'

'It was.'

'You described me as the girl whose outfit matched her hair. No wonder you knew my full name today.'

Her mind was jolted again. 'You made Ralph write that note before he left the convention, then you sent him back to London. Which means you knew all the time he wouldn't be coming here. Yet you came yourself.'

'I had the impression Ralph was about to make a fool of himself over a woman—one, moreover, he was hiding from his family. I wanted to take a close look at that woman. I'm glad I did. I was right in my assumption about you.'

'What about me?' Fran knew she sounded as bewildered as she felt.

'Hard, calculating.' His eyes were as cold now as they had been warm before the 'phone rang.

'But I'm not either of those things,' Fran objected.

'Coldbloodedly insinuating yourself into my fool stepbrother's emotions.'

'You've misunderstood the whole situation. All along, Ralph's accepted "no involvement" quite happily. He wasn't ready, he said, for any deep relationship. He had a career to make for himself.'

'A man doesn't reckon marriage as a barrier to a career as a woman might. In the eyes of society, it enhances it. And you're not a fool—you must have had some idea how he felt about you. So I don't accept your contention.'

'I'm not arguing with you,' she insisted. 'I'm telling you the truth. He accepted the condition.'

'In that case, why did Ralph tell me just now that he loved you?'

'He can't love me! Up to now, we've had little more than a brother–sister relationship.'

'Up to now?' he took her up. 'Meaning that you've been dictating the pace and that this weekend you were prepared to take the first step along the road to your ultimate goal, marriage to a Dowd?'

'I tell you,' her voice rose in her effort to set the

record straight, 'I never intended marrying Ralph—or anyone. Nor take part in any relationship where love is involved. He understood that.'

She looked into his cold blue eyes and remembered the glitter she had seen there that morning after she had fought free of his embrace. He must have been testing her even then!

He leaned on his arm on the back of a chair, still looking at her.

'So what terrible thing happened to you to cause you to become so hard? Left stranded by a boyfriend?'

The derision in his tone made her turn on him fiercely. 'No! My parents' divorce was finalised a few weeks ago, that's what happened. No one can watch the break-up of their parents' marriage without feeling their whole world has gone dark.'

'Give it time. Someone will switch the light back on.'

'Never. I feel as if I've been pushed off a diving board and hit the hard, tiled bottom. Their parting has ruined my feeling of security in any relationship.'

'Which means you've sworn never to let yourself fall in love. Right?' His faint smile held mockery.

'Yes, I have. After watching my parents tear themselves apart, I've vowed I'm not going to get near enough to any man and let the same shattering thing happen to me.'

'So Ralph would have been just one more in a long line of discarded men.'

'You can think that if you like. If I tell you I've been keeping men out of my life for the past year or two, you wouldn't believe me, would you?'

He did not answer, but let his eyes drift over her, returning to her face. 'Your mouth was ready enough to receive mine this morning.'

'I took your kisses for what they were,' she declared,

'fun, spontaneous and meaningless. That was how you intended them, wasn't it?'

'Know something?' His eyes were speculative now. 'I could do with a woman like you in my life.'

The jerk her heart gave made Fran hold her throat. 'Too bad I'm not on offer.'

He went on as if he hadn't heard. 'I married a woman for whom I had some feeling and who I thought returned that feeling.'

'You're married?' Fran asked, then wondered why her fingers were making indentations in her throat.

'We were very close for two years, then we decided to make it legal. She knew I wanted children, eventually. On the day of the wedding, she bolted. Couldn't face the responsibilities of marriage and motherhood, she said. She waited until after the ceremony to get out of my life—a nice little turn of the screw.'

'I wouldn't do such a thing,' Fran responded, eyes wide. 'Which is why I said I'd never marry.'

'Not even for the maintenance payments?'

'How could she have expected those after what she did to you?'

'Expect them or not, she got them after the divorce. We'd shared a couple of eventful years. That was four years ago. She remarried. Financially, she's off my back.' He approached slowly, eyes narrowing on to Fran's face. 'You're twenty-four. You've made your journalistic way upwards through Dowd Wideworld's various magazine publications. You've shown considerable promise, tackling each job with enthusiasm and energy. You're reliable, your work is consistent, you get on well with your colleagues.'

'You're talking like a job reference,' she jeered.

'Exactly. After seeing you at the convention, I called London. At my request, my secretary read out relevant details from your personal file.'

'To check whether I was suitable for Ralph?'

His eyes narrowed further at her indignation. 'No. To see if you were suitable for me. You see,' his hand rested on top of her head, forcing it backward so that she looked up at him, 'I was *coldly* and *dispassionately* deciding whether you would fit the role of my wife.'

Her head twisted under his restraining hand, but she did not succeed in dislodging it.

'You don't like it much, do you,' he sneered, 'when the tables are turned on you?' He removed his hand and Fran's head jerked forward painfully. 'You object to the calculated approach when you're the one to whom it's applied.' He watched her rub her neck. 'I'm asking you, calculatedly and detachedly, if you'll be my wife.'

His words were clipped, his eyes cold. Fran found herself searching in the handsome, hard face of Evan Dowd for the warm, laughing person that had been Johnny Black. She knew she was wasting her time. She told herself that that personality had been as much a figment of her imagination as the name Johnny had been of Evan Dowd's.

But his question, which was only just making an impact, had been real enough. He was only joking, she reminded her hammering heart, yet there wasn't the slightest trace of humour in his expression.

'No!' The word came out like a cry, as if he had threatened her. 'Thank you,' she added more quietly.

'Think about it,' he suggested, watching her. 'Tell yourself you'll never again receive such a proposal of marriage. That any other man would tag on that he loved you, needed you, wanted you in his life as his partner and loving companion. You know,' his mouth twisted, 'all that rubbish a man tells a woman he's in love with. Don't forget that I have just as jaundiced a view as you have of that love you despise and distrust.

Remember, too, that I'm never again going to let emotion cloud my view of a woman. Nor am I ever again letting myself suffer pain at any woman's hands.'

Fran shook her head, saying, 'It's still no.'

'It's an answer I'm not prepared to take,' he stated levelly. 'The fact is that I need a wife. An opportunity like this may not occur a second time—the chance to marry a woman who doesn't care a damn for me, nor I for her. I suggest you think about it.'

He turned away, taking up his discarded jacket and carrying it towards the stairs.

'I told you,' she called after him, 'marriage is out.'

He halted, turning with a broad, derisive smile. 'Then live with me. Be my woman.'

Her heart somersaulted at the outrageous suggestion. But, she heard her other self argue, you haven't ruled that out, have you? Only a loving relationship . . . She listened to her lips forming the words, 'No again. Thanks.'

'I'll give you twenty-four hours.' His bold stare swept her shape, his mouth curved faintly on a reflective smile, but his face gave away nothing of his thoughts. 'It's worth waiting that long.'

'I'll be gone by then.' She consulted her watch. 'In fact, I'll pack and leave this evening.'

'Got a seat booked on a flight out tonight?' He watched her shake her head. 'Then it's too late, isn't it? You were going back tomorrow evening with Ralph? Then stick to that particular flight.'

He climbed the stairs, his strides deep and quick. Fran watched him go, knowing he had talked sense. He had won thus far. But no more victories to him, she vowed.

In her room, Fran heard him moving around. The shower hissed and gurgled, his voice lifted over it in song, the words only slightly less bawdy than those he had sung earlier down in the ski room.

The words drifted to her: When a woman lies beside a man and offers him love for money, she lies with her eyes, she lies with her lips, she lies with her . . .

Fran clapped her hands over her ears, then her eyes came open wide. It was Johnny Black come back. He'd turned back into Johnny . . . She wrenched open her door, only to see him moving into his room, a towel wrapped around his hips, his strong legs running with water.

Before she could move, he turned to close his door, seeing her. The blue eyes held hers, dark with amusement, but his question shot across the dividing corridor. 'Changed your mind? What's it to be— woman or wife?'

Her stare dropped of its own accord to take in his lean length, the damp whorls of hair on his chest. 'Neither,' she answered, wondering why her voice had sounded hoarse, then shut the door on his broad, derisive smile.

Why don't I stop deluding myself, she thought angrily. And what was so special anyway, about that non-existent creature called Johnny? Her thoughts came to a crash stop, before they could conjure him up yet again for an excrutiating analysis of that imagined man's assets.

Ten minutes later, the door slammed and her heart with it. The place was empty and unfamiliar, yet she dared not set foot outside for fear of getting lost in the surrounding snow wastes.

For the second time that day, she counted the slow-moving minutes. It was in the early hours that she heard his movements again. There were people with him. A woman's voice, a man's, then another woman's. Then Evan's laughter, so like Johnny's, almost shaking the chalet. Music played, voices were raised over it. Sleep was impossible, so Fran sat curled on her bed, a jacket around her shoulders, trying to read a book.

She awoke with a start, the light too bright, making her cover her eyes. Her hand reached for the book, encountered stranger's hands and froze rigid with fear. When she heard the mocking, 'Waiting for me?' she uncovered her eyes and stared at the man with black hair and blue eyes that glinted down at her.

'You kept me awake,' she threw at him, fatigue undermining her control.

'If I'd known I'd have invited you to the party. How could I have introduced you, do you think?' He dwelt on her short cotton nightdress, the bare, silky shoulders, the deep brown hair loose down her back. 'A fashion journalist I fancied and picked up on the slopes? My hideaway woman?'

'Will you stop trying to make me feel small? Please, I'm tired. Will you let me sleep now?' With the heel of her hand she rubbed her eyes, then stared heavily up at him. There were dark shadows around his neck and chin. She wondered idly if he needed to shave twice a day, then stopped her thoughts at source. She'd never know the answer to such a personal question.

A hand was pulling back the cover, another was around her waist and lifting her into bed. She shivered at the contact. 'Will you stop touching me!' It had come out as an appeal instead of anger.

The knowing eyes rested on her but he did not break contact. She lay on her side, staring up at him. He ran his palm down her arm as it rested outside the cover. Her skin came alive under his touch and she tensed to stop herself responding.

'Will——' she moistened her lips, 'will you close the door behind you when you go out, please?'

It was a whisper, another plea and he laughed, putting back his head. 'Another way of saying "no".' He opened the door wide. 'Sleep now. Give me the answer I want tomorrow.' He turned out the light.

'I'll give you your answer now,' she murmured sleepily. But try as she might, she could not get her tired tongue around the words 'no thank you' that hung suspended in her mind.

CHAPTER THREE

IT was ten o'clock when she awoke, surprisingly fresh. Half sitting up, she listened to silence. Opening the door, she looked across the corridor. Evan's room was empty. Her expectations took a dive as she realised he must have gone skiing without her.

In the fridge, she found a carton of milk. This she poured and drank, eating some crispbread and honey. The outside world beckoned and she was determined this time not to ignore its call. While she was there— only a few more hours—she would make the most of the situation and look around her. That afternoon, she would pack her things and make her way to the coach which Ralph had told her they would catch back to the city and on to the airport.

Fran pulled on layers of clothes, topping them with her anorak. Her breath hung on the cold morning air and her booted feet sank into the snow which covered the path from the chalet. Halfway down, she stopped and looked around her. The sight of the tops of fences and bushes pushing through the snow-crust told a tale of how many everyday things were buried beneath her feet. In a dream she wandered round the wide-roofed shops, buying a souvenir or two and pushing them into her pockets. There were people everywhere, the brilliant colours of their clothes vying for attention with the illuminated signs which, even in the daylight, flashed brightly.

Fran noticed after a while that the shoppers had been joined by skiers carrying their equipment. It seemed that the first ski session of the day was over.

All the men, she observed, were tall; all the women were graceful and attractive. Amused by the thought, she told herself that it couldn't really be so. But the 'beautiful people' did seem to abound in that ski resort, she concluded, and turned to stare at a particularly handsome man with a laughing group. His profile flashed round and she saw with a shock that it was Evan Dowd, walking beside a tall blonde woman who shouldered her skis like a professional.

Withdrawing her eyes, Fran turned to look where she was going, only to feel a staggering blow on the side of her head and to find herself falling. The hard-packed snow held no gentleness as her hip and shoulder hit the ground, and she heard a cry which she did not realise came from her.

There were shouts and running feet and a sound like a voice saying, 'Let me get to her, will you?' Then she heard nothing at all.

It could have been hours or only a few moments later when she heard voices raised in apology and question. When she felt damp and melting snow beneath her outspread fingers, she knew she was lying in the busy street where she had fallen.

'No, no,' a familiar voice said, 'she's my responsibility. She belongs to the Dowd chalet. Not far . . . That's okay, I'll carry her. If you'll bring my skis . . .'

It was so much easier, Fran found, to let her body relax into the rhythm of the striding body against which she was held. She must, she realised, have slept a little, since she stirred and found a warm softness beneath her head and limbs.

'It's one of the biggest dangers of a skiing holiday.' It was a man talking and she opened her eyes to see who he was addressing. Was that attractive blonde

woman there? What connection did she have with
Evan Dowd?

'What is?' Had that been her own voice, and if so,
where was she?

'Getting hit on the head—off the slopes—by
someone else's skis. Trust you to become the victim of
such an accident.'

'I'm not usually accident prone,' she argued,
realising as she talked that it was Evan Dowd—who
else?—provoking her.

Looking around, she saw she was in his bedroom. It
seemed he was alone.

Inconsequentially, she asked, 'Where's that beautiful
blonde who was walking beside you?'

He smiled enigmatically. He sat on the large bed,
his hand resting lightly over hers. 'Is that who you
were craning your neck to look at?'

Fran thought, but did not say aloud, No, it was you
who caught my attention. You're too good-looking to
be true. She opted for silence, waiting with a strange
apprehension, to be told the woman's identity.

'That was Willa Hemming, a fashion model.'

Fran nodded, relief giving her a little colour. The
movement also brought a shaft of pain to her head.

'My ex-wife.'

The additional piece of information banished the
relief at once. 'Did you know she would be here?'

'Coincidence. At least, it was from my angle. In the
past, we came skiing here. Whether that caused her to
come in the hope of finding me, I don't know.' He
paused. 'She's after a reconciliation.'

The pain ran in circles round Fran's head as she lifted
it sharply. 'Which solves your problem of finding
yourself a wife. She's there waiting for you, ready made.'

'There's one minor obstacle,' he observed dryly.
'She's already married—to another man.'

'That's easily solved, isn't it,' Fran heard herself saying as if it were another person speaking. 'She's probably getting a divorce, otherwise she wouldn't have suggested your coming together with her again. It's only a matter of time.'

It was, she decided, rather like driving a nail into one's own head—speaking against her will and, surprisingly, she had to admit it, against her own interests. It was the pounding ache where the skis had hit her that was making her think these foolish thoughts. It was that ache, too, which, when he asked yet again, 'Changed your mind?' made her answer, almost involuntarily, 'Yes.'

'Yes?' He paused. 'You're agreeing to become my wife?'

'No.' She lifted her head, then wished she hadn't. 'Of course not. I'm still saying no.' She closed her eyes, lifting a hand to her head. 'Please let me sleep.' Moving only her eyes, she watched him rise from the bed and leave.

The room, she observed, was as untidy as it had been the first time she had seen it. There was the feel about it of Johnny Black, not Evan Dowd. The standards of that autocratic man were too inflexible to allow such everyday disorder to exist.

There were voices in the room when she woke up again, speaking quietly. Someone was wrapping a band round her arm, pumping air, listening, and removing the instrument. The words were in French, she discerned, and the stranger was plainly a doctor.

When she opened her eyes, he smiled encouragingly down at her. She nodded, although she could understand only a few words. 'You will be better soon,' she was able to translate. 'Rest . . . a day or two. The pain in your head will go . . . *Au revoir, mademoiselle*.' The doctor inclined his head.

'*Merci, monsieur, au revoir, monsieur,*' Fran said, pleasing the visitor, who repaid the compliment by adding, in English, 'You will soon be well.'

Evan Dowd accompanied the doctor out of the room and Fran became aware that the ski pants she had been wearing had been removed. They were on a chair across the room. It embarrassed her to think of her host easing her out of them. It must, she thought smiling, have been Evan who had folded them so neatly. Johnny would have dropped them to the floor.

Then she sobered. It won't do, she told herself, to go on thinking of the man in whose bed she was lying as having two personalities. It was time to face the fact that the man she had first met the evening she arrived had no existence separate from Evan Dowd. He had imagined up Johnny, played out the role of Johnny and invented every nuance and angle of his character.

'You're to rest. Doctor's orders.' Evan stood in the doorway, tall and unsmiling.

Fran struggled to sit half upright. 'It's not possible. I'm going home this afternoon. But,' she sank down tiredly, 'thanks for getting medical advice.'

'You're staying right here.' He approached, arms folded.

'That's impossible. I have to be back at work tomorrow. I've got a couple of important appointments. I've waited weeks for them. I *have* to go.'

'Your deputy can take them over.'

Fran did not object out loud to the suggestion. She kept it to herself. Putting on a smile, she asked, 'Are you going skiing this afternoon?'

'If I am, you're not going with me.'

'Of course not,' she agreed quickly—too quickly, it seemed, from Evan's expression. Suspicion narrowed his eyes, tautened his answering smile. 'I'm—I'm hungry, Evan.' Had she diverted his mind from its speculation about her possible action when he had gone out?

By the flickering of his eyelids, she wondered if she had, but crossed her fingers secretly. He gave her a light lunch, saying he had already eaten. He left her, having made her comfortable and she heard his voice from the living room.

Putting aside the tray, she rested back against the pillows. Was he talking to his ex-wife, arranging a meeting? Would he come back, telling her to forget the proposal he had made, because he was prepared to wait for his ex-wife to get a divorce?

She closed the door on her thoughts. Evan Dowd's private life was no concern of hers. He had been joking when he had asked her to be his wife. She had been completely serious, hadn't she, when she had refused?

When the main entrance door slammed in the distance, she pushed her legs free of the bedcover and tried to hurry to the window. She had been too slow. Evan had gone. His footsteps must have been among the many that punctuated the deep, white snow cover leading to and from the chalet.

If I can make the effort, Fran thought, I'll get into my clothes.

Dredging energy from somewhere deep inside her and forcing herself to ignore the hammering in her head, she left Evan's bedroom and slipped across to her own. She pulled on warm slacks and a couple of layers of bulky tops. Her suitcase was only half unpacked and she filled it with the rest of her belongings.

Checking on her tickets and supply of money, she lifted into place the hood of her quilted jacket and wound a thick scarf round her neck. Her boots were only ankle-high, but she knew they would at least keep her feet dry.

Making the main entrance, she closed it quietly behind her. Her breath was suspended on the freezing air. The sun had sunk lower in the clear sky than she had expected, but she estimated that she would reach the coach in the town centre before it set.

It was her legs that threatened to let her down. They were heavy and reluctant to lift clear of the white and sparkling crust beneath them. The aching soreness at the side of her head slowed her progress and she wished she had remembered to ask Evan for tablets to ease the pain. Her suitcase was surely heavier than when she had come?

When her leg sank into the snow to more than knee-height, she cried out. Her other leg, trying to find a harder surface, sank in beside it. Her hand had slipped from its hold on the suitcase, which landed some distance away. She drew a couple of laboured breaths and looked about her. 'Please?' she called. Then a wavering, 'Help!'

Giant footsteps approached from behind. She strained to look over her shoulder. 'I thought you'd gone out,' was all she could think of saying to the man in the scarlet and yellow anorak and dark ski pants who was striding hugely towards her.

'I know you did. I guessed your crazy plan and hung around for you.' He stood above her, gloved hands thrust in pockets, regarding her with a kind of gloating amusement. 'You look like a doll that's fallen from a Christmas tree.'

'Except that this snow is certainly not artificial,' she retorted. 'Please, Mr Dowd,' she held out her arms, 'will you get me out? It's soaking through my clothes. And my head's aching.'

He scrutinised her pale, upturned face. 'I could say get yourself out of it, especially as you disobeyed doctor's orders and mine.' Something in her face must have stirred him. He relented and crouched down, fastening his hands around her waist and easing her out.

He set her down and went to retrieve her case. She stood shivering, hand to her head. He returned and she lifted a distraught face to him. She saw his grim expression and looked away towards the mountains. They were as likely to comfort her as this man was.

Arms came round her, scooping her towards broad shoulders and a chest like a stone wall. 'There's no need,' she protested, but could not stop her shaking hands from gripping him.

Balancing her on his knee, he bent to pick up her case, then made his way to the chalet. 'You didn't get far, did you, trying to escape from me?' he jeered, his deep, heated breaths fanning Fran's face.

'You made sure of that,' she murmured against the softness of his jacket. 'Plus the conditions.' Her waving hand indicated the white, forbidding landscape.

'You surely took those into account when you made your getaway plans?'

'Not really,' she sighed. 'When Ralph and I discussed my visit, we assumed he would be with me.'

His jaw hardened against the top of her head. 'Forget my stepbrother,' he said on a note of anger. 'The only Dowd you have to reckon with now is me.'

He entered the chalet and lowered her to the floor, bending to switch on an electric heater. 'Get those damp things off,' he directed, looking at her wet, clinging pants.

She nodded. 'In my bedroom.'

'Shy?' he mocked, helping her to remove her jacket. 'I've already seen most of your body. Or did you think I called in a nurse this morning to remove your trousers before putting you into my bed?'

Her sudden bright colour amused him, but as she made for the door, he moved quickly, putting himself in her way. 'If you're going to any bedroom, it'll be mine.'

Baffled, and a little anxious, she asked, 'Why?'

'Because that's your ultimate destination. I told you, I'm not intending to pass up the opportunity of having as a wife a woman who's willing—which I know you are—and,' his gaze dropped to her thighs which shaped the legs of her wet trousers, 'feminine, yet asks nothing from me emotionally. As I'll ask nothing of her in that way.'

Shaking her head, she said, 'How many times do I have to tell you "no"?'

'I could say you're staying until you say "yes".'

Her eyes widened. 'A form of kidnap? Someone in your position wouldn't stoop to that?' She made the statement into a question because she wasn't sure of the answer. He gave her the one she dreaded.

'It's precisely someone of my financial and business status who can choose to do such a thing. But you've put it a little strongly. I haven't kidnapped you. You're free to go just as soon as you give me the answer I want.'

She challenged, eyes overbright, 'I could always say yes, then after you'd released me, renege on it.'

She had trodden on the tail of his anger without doubt. He closed the gap between them and encircled her with one arm. 'Oh no,' he growled. 'I've been bitten that way once. Never again. The moment you agree, it'll be almost an accomplished fact. Notices will be put into newspapers, announcements made both inside and outside the company, relatives informed.'

She turned her head away, shutting her eyes as her world rocked at the prospect.

His free hand stroked her hair lightly. 'I'm offering you not only marriage, but status, financial security, whatever you ask for. Just name it.'

Her eyes flashed open. 'Freedom—from you.'

He laughed and there was a touch of menace in it. 'That you won't get. Until you marry me. Then you can wander the world, if you like.' He held her slightly away and his eyes weaved a course over her. 'That is, whenever I don't need you.'

'Please, Mr Dowd——' she started to struggle from his hold.

'You called me Evan earlier today.'

Her head began to throb. 'I'll call you anything you want, if—if you'll let me rest somewhere. Please——' she took a breath, 'Evan.'

He let her go and there was concern in his eyes. 'Your head hurts?' She nodded. 'I'll get you something to dull the pain.' He returned with water and a towel slung over his shoulder, waiting while she took the tablets. Then he crouched, before she could object, to find her waistband and peel away the wet trousers.

'Please don't,' she protested faintly, but felt unequal to any struggle with him. Then he used the towel on her hips and legs in strong strokes. Her flesh grew warm with the powerful friction. It was the stimulation of her circulation, she argued with herself, it was nothing to do with the intimacy of his action. But all the reason in the world could not prevent the leap of her pulses as he firmed his hold high on her inner leg. 'Please, Evan,' she urged through tight teeth.

He looked up without relaxing his grip. There was a passing surprise in his eyes, which swiftly turned to comprehension. He dropped the towel and stood up, putting his hand round her waist. 'Is that the way the wind blows,' he commented, tipping her chin and looking sleepily into her wide eyes. 'So be it.'

His mouth rested on hers, taking to itself a light kiss, then lifted and descended from one side of her lips to the other. He paused, eyes glinting and asked, 'What should I thank for this—the painkillers? Is that the only way you can bring yourself to bear my touch?'

She smiled, lowered her eyes and shook her head. She could not tell him that her reactions had even surprised herself. He seemed to be waiting for an answer.

'You're——' she moistened her lips. 'You must know that you're——' she fixed her eyes on the geometrical pattern on his round-necked sweater, 'you're attractive to women. My—my responses to you were completely primitive.'

'Over which you had no control?'

Why, she wondered, were his eyes so brilliant? 'That's right,' she answered, then immediately regretted it.

'Ah, now I have it. I know the pathway to your door. And,' he hooked a finger in one of the button fastenings on her jacket, 'if you hadn't been almost knocked cold this morning by those damned skis, I'd follow that path and hammer your door down.'

Her skin crept, then burned at the thought. Her head moved negatively. 'I wouldn't allow it.'

He tugged at the button hole, unfastening it. 'You're not talking to my shy, good-mannered stepbrother now. I know women's ways——'

'But,' she cut in, 'I'm not any woman.'

His eyelids flickered. 'You certainly are not. You're a puzzle, an unknown quantity, most of all, a challenge.'

'I'm very tired.' The words came out spontaneously.

Evan's head went back in laughter. 'After my build-up, what an anticlimax!' He sobered and his hand skimmed her hair, fastening on her top-knot. 'I can tell you one thing. Now I've found you, I'm not letting you go. Not yet, not for a long time to come.'

She guessed his meaning and broke free. 'I said no, no!' There was fear in her voice. Her heart was hammering and she felt trapped. Swinging towards the door, she felt the room begin to sway and she started falling. Strong hands caught her, pushed her head down and told her to be still. She hung over his arm as it pressed against her breasts, then he lifted her slowly upright. She felt like a puppet in his hands.

He had tugged at the only comfortable chair in the living-room, making it into a bed. Now, she lay looking up at him. 'Don't you understand?' she pleaded. 'I have to go home.'

'Did I forget to tell you? You're not going.'

'Of course I am. I said I had work to do tomorrow.'

'And I'm saying I called London and spoke to your deputy. She's coping with your work over the next few days.'

'You spoke to Judy? What will she think now? You had no right.'

'No?' It was one of the top men of Dowd Wideworld talking. 'I had every right, I think. Don't you?'

Fran looked at him suspiciously. 'As a member of the Dowd family?'

'In my capacity as chief executive of the company.' It was almost dark, but she could see the frost in his eyes. 'Stop fighting me, will you?'

There was a rough huskiness in the voice that made Fran try to see its owner's face. The small light that remained highlighted the broad forehead, the hard cheekbones, the stubborn chin.

She nodded but doubted if he could see her assent.

'For now,' she tacked on, sighing. Footsteps moved away across the thinly carpeted floor.

'Feeling better?' Evan stood beside the chair, looking at her.

It seemed no more than a few minutes since she closed her eyes, but the clock on a shelf told her it was more than an hour. 'Thanks, yes,' she answered.

He flicked her face with a look. 'Judging by the smile and the bright eyes, back to better than normal.' He lifted off the rug he had placed over her.

He wore a dark blue leisure shirt with buttoned pockets, while a belt spanned his lean waist. His hair held an after-shower dampness. Fran frowned. 'Are you going somewhere?'

'Aprés-ski,' he told her. 'It's very popular—discos, restaurants, milk bars, you can take your choice. Socialising at a chosen hotel.'

'Sounds fun.' Fran tested her head and discovered the pain had gone. 'Could I come?'

'You have to rest. Doctor's instructions. There are books, magazines.'

'I don't want to be left alone! I mean,' seeing his raised eyebrows, 'I'm feeling much better.'

'The pain-killers are still working.'

'Even if they are, I don't see why I can't go out. I might as well sample the pleasures as well as the pain,' she touched her head and made a face, 'of a ski resort. I won't be coming this way again.'

'You think not? I can see no reason why we shouldn't take a few weekend breaks here after we're married.'

Her heart bumped at his casual reference to a relationship which could never be and even if it could, one that she would not want. 'I wish you would stop making jokes at my expense.'

'Believe me, Francesca, joking I am not.' His hand came out, offering her leverage to rise. He hauled her upright, putting an arm round her to steady her.

'I'm okay,' she said with irritation. 'I can stand on my own two feet.' Her eyes sought his. 'Please let me come.'

'How shall I describe you to the people we meet?' His two arms met around her waist.

She pushed back her hair, shaking her head. 'As a friend? Does it matter?'

'Friend, hmm? That's a start. And yes, it does matter,' he added, without explaining why.

The hotel resembled a large chalet and the entrance was beneath a canopy. In the reception area there were coloured lights and baskets of flowers. Everywhere there was wood, polished and bright. Woven rugs were scattered, low seats held sprawling guests.

As they entered, Fran saw the reason why Evan had said it mattered how he introduced her. On a high stool, legs bent to rest on its supporting bar, was a woman with long, blonde hair. Her turquoise coloured dress clung to her body, leaving her arms and shoulders bare. Fran had glimpsed her that day walking at Evan's side. It was Evan's former wife.

The room was spacious, with low tables and soft lighting. Some guests had chosen to sit at the bar while others gathered in groups. Ignoring the cool stare of the woman to whom he had once been married, Evan urged Fran towards a long table.

He sat her down and pulled his own chair tightly to hers. He had bought her a drink which, he said, was only mildly alcoholic. 'Make the most of it,' he told her. 'It's got to last you the whole evening.'

'But I——' she began to protest, then realised the reason for his caution. He was right. It was inadvisable to mix pain-killers with alcohol.

There were laughing people the length of the table. They called out to Evan, waving their arms, lifting glasses. They were, to Fran's bemused eyes, all good-looking. The women were tanned and attractive, their clothes bright and well-cut. The men, like Evan, were bronzed and fit, wearing patterned sweaters and open-necked shirts.

Evan Dowd, she thought, fitted in with such people. Their speech was educated, their financial status high; confidence flowed in their conversation, their tone of voice. The man beside Fran asked where she was staying and was the hotel she'd chosen comfortable?

Evan, who had put his arm round her waist, leaned forward and answered, 'She's staying at the Dowd chalet. I think she'd agree,' he lifted her chin with hard fingers, 'that I'm making her as—comfortable as I possibly can?'

It was a question directed at her. His eyes held hers, too, and lurking in their depths Fran saw a warning light. Play your part, they were saying, or else . . .

'It's a fine hotel,' she remarked, gazing as though love-struck into her tormentor's eyes, 'with a five-star owner in charge.' She laughed into his face and removed his hand from her chin, putting it to her lips. Her brows lifted, asking silently, Is my acting good enough for you? It worried her just a little that she found the part of woman to his man so easy to play.

His lips nuzzled her ear, and there was a whisper of 'Hussy! I'll teach you a lesson when we get home.'

She tried to free herself. His threat might have been just an attempt to put her in her place, but the fact that he could make it showed how familiarity was growing between them, even if it was only in the mind. He let her go, removing his arm. Fran discovered inside herself a niggling sense of disappointment. To rid herself of the panic this self-revelation created, she reached out for her glass and tipped back her head to swallow the liquid. The whole action had been too hasty and her body's reaction was to cough until the tears came.

Her brimming eyes turned to Evan in mute appeal but it was not his hand that tapped her on the back, it was the young man's on her other side. 'Thanks,' she managed, turning a grateful smile on to him. Her resentful stare came back to rest on Evan, but she found no sympathy there, only an aloofness that chilled.

His attention was attracted by a woman called Liz across the narrow table, and Fran turned to the man who had just come to her rescue. He was in conversation with his other neighbour and Fran was left to sip at her drink in silence.

Her back was to the woman called Willa, but she could hear her husky voice and silky laughter. A powerful feeling clutched at Fran's inside, but when she tried to analyse its source, her hand came out again for the glass. It was the events of the day, she told herself, that had caused that feeling.

'So you're in the fashion business, too.' The husky voice was right behind her, making the skin of her neck creep. Evan had stopped talking, but did not turn at the sound of his ex-wife's voice.

Fran knew she could not ignore her, however, and looked round, assuming her outgoing, journalist's personality. 'How did you know?' she asked the slender, fair-haired model, then, as the woman moved round, caught her breath at her flawless beauty.

It was a face she had seen in the fashion columns of newspapers, on magazine covers, and full-length, modelling clothes on the inside pages. If this was truly Evan Dowd's kind of female, then she, Fran, stood no chance of holding him, even in a relationship based on no more than physical attraction. Does it worry me? she wondered, and found herself answering that it did. It's the underlying insecurity, she told herself quickly, which my parents' break-up has caused.

'Evan told me,' Willa Hemming answered.

So they've been talking about me, Fran thought with an angry glance at the man beside her. He had risen and was looking from one woman to the other. Fran swore she could see amusement in his face.

'Willa's temporarily free of assignments,' Evan said casually. 'I suggested she should speak to you.' Seeing Fran's puzzlement, he added, 'About modelling work.'

'You want me to offer your ex——' she checked, 'Miss Hemming a job on *Woman's Choice*?'

The chief executive of the publishing company raised his eyebrows. 'I fail to see why not.'

'But, Evan, the people we use are much younger——' There was anger in Evan's glance. 'I'm sorry,' she amended, 'I meant in a different age group. *Woman's Choice* features the more casual styles, the kind that are easy to wear. Miss Hemming is——' Fran moistened her lips; two pairs of rebuking eyes upon her were hard to take, 'is very—attractive, that goes without saying.' I'm floundering, she thought, any minute now I'll sink without trace in the current these two are producing between them. 'But she's too ... more sophisticated in her style than *Woman's Choice* requires in its models.'

'I insist,' Evan said quietly.

'But——' She felt in his compelling gaze the power he was wielding, that of his high position in the company. 'You'll—you'll have to ask the editor of the magazine,' Fran ended helplessly. 'She dictates its overall style.'

'It's you I'm telling,' he rebuked. 'As my future wife, you'll have influence beyond that of the editor.'

But I'm not your future wife ... The words screeched in her mind, but one look at Willa's furious face stopped her speaking them. All right, she thought, I'm being bitchy, but who can blame me? If it's gloves off for a fight over Evan Dowd, I'm going to use my advantage to the very limits. And I do have an advantage. In front of this stunning woman to whom he used to be married, he has named me as his wife-to-be. A small voice tried to remind her that she had no ambition to become Evan's wife, but she silenced it at once.

'Yes, darling,' she said with a flashing smile, putting her hands round Evan's upper arms, 'whatever you say. I'll certainly consider Miss Hemming when we're choosing clothes to feature in the magazine.'

'Good.' Evan pulled her arm through his and placed a tingling kiss on the side of her throat.

Two blazing green eyes met Fran's, then moved to rest on the tall man at her side. So Willa's jealous, Fran thought, experiencing a leap of pleasure in her sudden power over the sultry, angry woman.

For the rest of the evening, Evan's arm stayed around her waist. Fran found herself enjoying more and more the feel of him but it was only when she started to droop that she became relaxed against him. He looked down at her, mildly surprised.

'Just realised,' he prodded, 'you can't do without me after all?'

'No,' she retorted with disarming honesty, 'I'm only doing this to make your ex-wife jealous.'

'Frankly, my own,' he returned on a mocking note, 'I don't care what your motives are just as long as your body stays close to mine like this.'

'You are very loving this evening, Evan,' commented the young woman called Liz from across the table. 'I wish your *friend* would tell me her technique. I've lost count of the times I've tried to get a response from you.'

Evan looked with apparent fondness at the girl who half-reclined against his shoulder. 'Well, Francesca, what's your secret?'

She shook her head, too weary to supply a quick answer. 'I'm tired,' she said with finality.

Laughter greeted the statement and Evan commented in a drawl, 'Need she say more, Liz? She's given you her technique in a nutshell.'

He pulled her to her feet but she separated herself from him at once. She wanted to turn on him in anger at the implication he had made in public but the bright-eyed onlookers demanded that she keep up the pretence of being in love.

It was not until they arrived back at the chalet that the headache hit her again. She sank down on to the chair bed and covered her eyes. 'Sorry,' she mumbled, 'guess I shouldn't have gone with you, after all.'

'Lie back,' Evan commanded, but Fran shook her head. Her feet were hoisted unceremoniously to the chair extension and tugged so that she was lying flat despite her protests. 'I'll get you a warm drink.'

But she never had it, for the simple reason that she went to sleep. Waking in the night, she relished the comfort of the bed around her. Before she could wonder how she had got there, she was asleep again.

Much later, something disturbed her, a movement, an exhalation of breath. Then awareness returned and she stiffened with fright. It was not her bed! Evan lay beside her in the darkness.

CHAPTER FOUR

FRAN knew she must get away before he woke up. He stirred and she lay tense, waiting for him to settle down again. His arm came across her and his breath warmed her cheek. His shower-clean skin teased her nostrils, his chest hair prickled her bare arm. She wondered what she was wearing and discovered that this time when he had put her to bed he seemed to have decided that, for a night's rest, her top should be removed too. All she was wearing, she discovered, were her wispy bra and briefs.

His hand moved from her waist and found the softness of her breast.

'Please,' she whispered, trying to remove the moulding fingers. The more she attempted to prise his hand away, the more secure his hold became. She tried to shift towards the edge, but froze when his other hand moved down to her thigh.

A throbbing excitement was undermining her protective tension and she gasped as exploring fingers caressed her inner leg. 'No, no, Evan,' she pleaded, trying to dislodge his hand, but his hold firmed.

'Relax, enjoy it. I want you, woman.'

'No, no,' she repeated. 'My head ...' It was not hurting, but she had to stop him somehow.

He ignored her plea. His mouth found hers and his hands trailed paths of fire over her heated body. She found her arms going out to find him. Something beyond her was activating her instincts, instructing her in actions she had never made before. It's Johnny Black, she told herself, it's Johnny come back. She heard his name repeated in her mind, and he turned her round, removing the two wisps of covering he had allowed to remain.

Her mind was hazy now, her mouth moist and throbbing from his kisses. She wanted to withhold nothing from him, yet she had to tell him ...

'I've never made love before,' she heard herself say, her arms locked around his neck.

There was a disbelieving mutter of, 'You could have fooled me.' Then he moved on to her, weighing her down, but she rejoiced in the pressure of him, the feel of his hard-muscled limbs against hers. His hand eased a way between her thighs and she gasped as he took her. 'My God, she's right,' he said softly, his lips against her neck, 'but there's no drawing back now, Francesca.'

There was pain, but there was pleasure too, and she was lifted high on a cloud. But it came to an end and she heard him say, 'I don't want to hurt you any more than I already have.' Then he was gone from her and she lay spent in his arms.

It was not then that she counted the cost, it was later, when the morning sounds awoke her. Evan lay beside her, his eyes locked on the shadow patterns on the ceiling, his arms raised to support his head.

'Evan?' she whispered, looking into his face. It might have been carved from stone. He looked down at her as her chin rested on his chest, but there was no smile in his eyes. His mouth was a straight line.

Her heart sank slowly, then she shivered with cold and with the impact of what she had allowed to happen. It was like watching someone else, Fran thought, as he disentangled himself from her and swung from the bed. Was he so coldly dismissing towards all his women after the lovemaking was over? He stood straight and tall and for the first time she saw his nakedness, his powerful masculinity.

He looked at her again but she hid her eyes' brightness. Instinctively, she knew there was more to hide than that, not only from him but from herself, also. He turned away and went to the window, standing hands on hips. She looked at his back and knew how hard the man called Evan Dowd really was.

It hadn't been that man who had made love to her, she agonised, it had been Johnny Black. And she knew intuitively that she would never see Johnny Black's carefree eyes and laughing manner again.

Evan had found a robe and was pulling it on. He came across and looked down at her, and to her dismay, her body started reacting clamorously to the cool caress of his eyes.

'You called me Johnny, Johnny Black,' he said. 'Why?'

'I didn't—did I? I was thinking about him—you.' His dark brows rose in question. 'It—it made it easier,' she faltered, but felt so confused she did not know whether it was true or not.

'You could have said "no".'

'I did. It made no difference. You went right on.'

He lifted his dismissing shoulders. 'I was determined to have you. Now we've shared the act of lovemaking, you'll marry me as soon as possible after our return.'

He was speaking so detachedly of such an intimate act, she shuddered inwardly. Yet, she argued, wasn't that what she had wanted? No involvement of the emotions, nor would she allow herself to love a man ... But he had offered a love-free marriage, hadn't he?

'I told you,' she said, feeling curiously dispirited, 'I won't marry you. But thank you for asking.'

'I'm not asking. I'm telling you.' He was speaking quietly beside the bed. 'The act we've just shared has bound you to me even more firmly than I originally intended.'

'Without love.'

'Agreed. Without love. We've both learned from experience that emotional attachment doesn't possess the sticking power that's vital to keep a couple together. We will stay together without it.'

It was such an unequivocal statement that something made her want to object, to say there was a fault somewhere in his reasoning, but she couldn't find it in her to argue with him at that moment. Her head had started to ache again and she put her hand to it, turning away listlessly.

Had it all been a dream, she wondered, had that unbelievable merging of herself with Evan Dowd happened only in her mind? But her body could provide incontrovertible evidence that he had brought her to womanhood and physical maturity. So why did she feel so overwhelmingly that she wanted to cry?

Evan sat on the bed and stroked her hair. 'Your head—does it hurt?' he asked, his tone mild.

'A bit, but not so much that it will stop me getting dressed.'

He stood up and pocketed his hands. 'Is your mind clear and your reasoning functioning?'

'I think so,' she answered tentatively, 'in spite of what happened to me overnight.'

'Then listen to me. Tomorrow morning we'll return to London. I'll see to the formalities. The wedding will be quiet. You agree?'

'There's no need to be old-fashioned,' she protested. 'These days, a man doesn't need to propose to a woman just because he's made love to her.'

'In case you've forgotten, my proposal was made before we had sex.'

She shivered at his clinical approach. 'Is that the only way you can describe what happened between us?' she asked, dismayed. 'To me, it was an electrifying experience. It changed me—'

'Made you love the man who gave you that experience?' His eyes were watchful.

'You mean made me fall in love with you?' A sweep of feeling had her closing her eyes. She saw a face— that of the man who had first found her at the chalet, the man who had tried to teach her to ski, whose arms she had run into after her first solo effort. Then she looked up at the man beside her. 'Not you, I'm not in love with you,' she avowed. 'I couldn't be, could I? It's something that will never happen to me, I told you that.'

Why, she wondered, did that statement have a hollow ring? 'That lovemaking might have changed my body,' she added, 'but it hasn't changed my mind.'

His nod was brief, as if any fears he might have had were at rest.

'For a few days after our return,' he said, 'we'll live at my town house. After the ceremony, we'll continue to live there. It's central and within easy reach of the offices we work in.'

Fran sat up, dragging the sheet with her. 'I haven't agreed yet.'

'No?' Slowly, he reached out and took hold of the sheet. His strength was the greater and he forced the covering away to her waist. He sat sideways and pulled her into his arms, imprisoning her mouth and stroking her breasts until her body ached for fulfilment.

He took away his mouth and said, 'What's your answer now, mermaid? Will you marry me?'

'Please, will you stop,' she gasped, 'and let me try and think.'

'Sometimes,' he said, tipping back her head and placing quick kisses round her throat, 'it's better just to feel. Now, how do you *feel* about marriage to me?'

'My body says yes,' she gasped, 'but my reason says all this can't be happening. Three days ago I didn't even know you . . .'

'But I knew you.' He released her, stood up and seemed to withdraw into himself. 'I'd made it my business to find out everything about you. I even had a look at a photograph of you that Ralph had.'

'Ralph . . .' She frowned. 'What am I going to tell him?'

'You can forget my stepbrother.' His eyes were flint-like. 'This is between the two of us. You're not seeing him again until after we're married. Now,' his hands went to the tie belt of his robe, 'are you going to get yourself dressed or,' he bent over her, 'are we getting together again?'

She wrapped her arms around herself. 'As soon as you've gone, I'll have a shower.' He didn't move. 'Evan,' she whispered, 'it's all new to me. Will you try and understand? I'm not used to having a man around, a—a lustful man, too.'

'Provoking me, hmm?' His head went down and a light danced in his eyes. He pulled her from the bed and into his arms, 'Marriage to you,' he said, 'should be interesting, if nothing else. And don't break contact, Fran. What do you want me to say—that I'm deeply in love with you? That I won't be able to live without you? Because it wouldn't—'

'Be true,' she filled in, her hand reaching up and covering his mouth. 'I know, but— just don't say it. A girl has her pride. I'll—I'll marry you, for the simple reason that——' Why, she wondered, am I hesitating? '—that, as you said, it will be a long time before I find a man who doesn't demand my—' her tongue tip ran round her dry lips, 'my undying devotion.' She tugged at a bed cover and wrapped it round herself. 'I'm going to my room to dress.'

She flung him a smile, but she looked back and judged from his expression that his feelings had turned cold.

'I'm skiing this afternoon.' Evan stood at the door of Fran's bedroom, shirtsleeves rolled, hands on hips. 'Will you come?'

He couldn't, Fran thought, be more different if he tried from the man who had made love to her in the early hours. She had been lying on the bed in her own room, trying without success to get out of her mind the shape of his face, the piercing blue of his eyes. It was because he was her first lover, she told herself, no other reason.

He suggested that she should rest her head, as the doctor had prescribed. She had agreed, not so much because her head was troubling her as through a wish to remove herself from Evan's presence. Every time he came near, she was horrified to discover that she wanted to make contact, to make him acknowledge that she meant something more to him than just a means of satisfying his desires.

Her heart jumped and an idea leapt into being with it. He was going to ski which, she calculated, meant that he would be out for an hour or two. She would seize her last chance to escape and that would require just a little pretence on her part.

'My head . . .' She waved her hand, indicating pain.

'If it goes on,' he said, straightening, 'I shall call the doctor back.'

'No!' Her eyes flew open. 'Thank you,' she added more quietly, hoping he had not noticed her alarm. 'It'll wear off soon, I'm certain.'

He lifted his shoulders in a Gallic-like shrug. 'I'll be off in half an hour. I won't disturb you again.'

'Thanks,' she answered, sighing and manufacturing a

quiet moan. He made a move to come across, but to
her relief, changed his mind and went away.

Thirty minutes later, she watched him tramp in his
heavy boots, skis weighting down wide shoulders,
towards the town centre, the bright colours of his
jacket brilliant against the snow's purity. Dialling the
airport's number, she managed to reserve a flight late
that evening to London.

The Heathrow crowds were muffled to their ears. It
was mid-March and, although warmer in temperature
than the ski resort Fran had left a few hours earlier,
the scene had none of its cheer and excitement.

She felt an emptiness inside as she turned the key
in the door of her two-bedroomed flat. It was, she
decided, a combination of tiredness and the knock
on the head, plus reaction to the events which she
still had not had time to put behind her. Far from
feeling dejected, she told herself she had just had a
lucky escape.

Drinking tea, she closed her eyes and pondered
over the terrible mistake she had so nearly let herself
be talked into making. If she had gone ahead and
become Evan Dowd's wife, she mused, there would
have been no doubt theat everything material that
she could ever have wanted would have been within
her grasp. And as for that missing ingredient—love,
well, that was something she would never expect,
nor ever want.

So what was wrong with marriage to Evan Dowd?
The question shot like a poisoned arrow into her
consciousness. Everything, she decided, getting to her
feet and clattering her cup in the kitchen sink. What
he had taken from her—and he had taken something
fundamental, there was no denying that—he could
keep. Will I, she wondered, feel embarrassed next
time I see him, after letting him make love to me?

How stupid can I get, she reproached herself. After walking out on him as she had, she would never see him again.

It was a week later, a week which Fran had used for getting up-to-date with her work both on the magazine and at home. She had returned to her normally tranquil existence. Whenever her thoughts had strayed back to the snow, the chalet and the man who sang doubtful songs in the ski room below, she forced them forward to the present.

In those seven days, there had not been a single 'phone call. He might, she caught herself thinking, have called once, if only to make sure she had arrived safely. Now, at the office, she stared out over London ten floors down and wondered what it really would have been like to be married to Evan Dowd. I'll never know, she told herself, then felt a sigh escape, a sigh she assured herself, of sheer relief.

It was time for lunch. Feeling in a self-indulgent mood, she had decided to patronise a better-than-usual restaurant and had consequently dressed with extra care. Emerging on to the busy street, she turned to walk towards the main shopping area.

A car door slammed and footsteps rang on the pavement. Instinctively, she began to hurry, but a hand fastened on her arm and swung her round. She opened her mouth to scream but a palm was slapped over it and a voice said,

'Walk, or else I'll carry you.'

It was the voice that had whispered 'I want you' in the darkness, coming from a man from whom she knew she just had to escape. 'I'll—I'll come,' she replied, darting glances around for someone to whom she could appeal for help, but he did not relax his hold as she had expected. 'Let me go,' she said, through teeth that were tight, otherwise they would have chattered.

The long legs beside hers closed the gap to the waiting car and she was pushed unceremoniously into the rear seat. Evan Dowd joined her there.

'What do you want from me?' she asked hoarsely as the driver, discreetly separated by a glass screen, pulled out into the stream of traffic. 'If it's an apology for leaving the chalet without letting you know, then I give it unreservedly. Now will you let me out of this car?'

'In my own good time.' The answer was clipped, the mouth that had delivered it a thin, straight line.

I must, she thought, get out of this. 'Th-thanks for looking after me at the chalet,' she stammered and saw that they were standing at traffic lights, 'but forget everything I said there, will you?'

She reached for the door handle but he had anticipated the movement. He tore her hand away, imprisoning it in his own. Cold blue eyes froze hers into a frightened stare. 'Where are we going?' she whispered, feeling her blood turn to ice around her heart.

He did not answer but reached into his pocket, pulling out a small box.

'I refuse to become engaged to you,' she stated fiercely. 'I revoke any promise I made at the chalet——' Then she gasped as she saw that the ring inside the box was a plain gold band.

She tried to free her hand, but he was pushing the ring on to her third finger, testing its size. 'Fine,' he commented crisply, putting it away.

The car turned into a parking place behind a large red-brick building. The driver held open the passenger door and she felt herself being urged out unceremoniously from behind.

'Good luck on your wedding day, Miss Williams,'

the driver said, smiling and standing smartly to attention.

Evan nodded and the car drove away. Stunned, Fran turned to him. 'What did he mean, what wedding day?'

'Ours,' he said shortly. 'In five minutes' time, we're getting married.' He must have seen the panic in her eyes and fixed them with his own, saying, 'Late as it is, I'm giving you the choice. Five minutes is more than enough to say "no". If the idea of marriage to me is entirely abhorrent to you, then turn around,' he made a circle with his finger, 'and get out of my life.'

Still his eyes held hers. They were a darker blue than usual, she perceived, unwavering, telling her volumes but she could not read a word.

'I want the decision this side of the ceremony, Francesca.' He spoke her name in his special way and her heart played tricks. 'If there's any running to be done, do it right now, before those vows are spoken. I've trodden this path, before, remember. My marriage to you is going to last. The reins will be slack. You go your way, I mine, but those reins will always be there to pull us back and hold us together.' A quick glance at his watch, then, 'What's your answer?'

Bewildered, she put a hand to her head. She looked down at her clothes. They were stylish, but they were not right for a wedding.

He seemed to guess her thoughts. 'You look beautiful, Francesca.'

'Th-thanks for saying that as though you meant it. But I——' First, she looked around and saw the latest bride and groom emerge and stand in the doorway around which climbing plants had been trained. They looked radiant and her heart went out to them. It's my wedding day, too, she told herself. She would be as radiant as that girl.

Then she looked at the man who was about to become her husband. 'It's my first marriage,' she told him, her smile flickering uncertainly, 'but I'm willing to do my very best to make it work.'

Fran stared through the car window, a bouquet of sweet-scented flowers lying on her lap. Evan had given them to her as they had emerged from the ceremony into the spring sunlight.

Two of his friends, an engaged couple, had attended the wedding and acted as witnesses. Afterwards, they had all shared a lavish meal at a famous London hotel.

Now, as she sat beside Evan in the driving seat, reality came rushing back and the doubts came crowding in. 'Everything's moving too fast,' she declared. 'I may be your wife now, but—but I don't feel I belong in your life.'

Evan glanced at her, brows raised, smile ironic. His hand rested over hers. 'It's a little difficult to prove here and now that that's exactly where you do belong, but,' his fingers tightened on hers, 'I promise you a demonstration when we get home.'

It's not my home, she wanted to tell him, but stayed silent.

'Where are we going?' she asked, after a while. 'I have to get back to the office.'

He smiled, glanced in the rear-view mirror and pulled out to overtake.

'I may not be a romantic, nor a lover who loves with his heart as well as his passion, but I'm darned if I'm going to deliver my bride back to her desk and her telephone on our wedding day. You can ring your deputy from the house and tell her to cover for you. And, please,' his hand lifted momentarily from the steering wheel, 'no argument. Accept the order from whence it came, the top.'

Fran was not sorry to subside and stifle her protest. Her feelings were at war inside her—those of bewilderment, excitement and a lingering apprehension—and she knew she would have to resolve the battle before she could think rationally enough for work.

'Will you tell me,' she said, 'when you're speaking as my boss, and when as my h——' He was her husband! Her wide eyes turned on him.

'Does the word stick in your throat? If so, I'm sorry, but I gave you the chance to say a final "no".'

'I know I agreed,' she protested, 'but it was under duress.'

He slowed for a road junction, then drove on. 'Duress? Come on, Francesca, be honest and admit it was the family name and the family money that proved too inviting to dismiss.'

'That's just not true,' she declared. 'If you think that, then you've misread my character.'

'So give me a better explanation.'

She sought for a reason. She had wanted to marry him and, strangely, her mind had been made up even before she saw that radiant couple emerging after their own wedding. What she didn't understand was why she had, in the end, accepted Evan's proposal of marriage.

The house came into view and Fran's lips parted. It stood some way back from a quiet road in a northern suburb. The building was of the Georgian period, painted white, with a balustraded porch and a heavy, panelled door.

Evan locked the car and joined her, using his key and motioning her inside. 'Yours as well as mine,' he commented with some irony. 'It won't bite.'

Fran entered, bemused, feeling that the house

would, like the events of the past two hours, fall on her
like a pack of cards. The day's happenings were
beginning to assume the unreality of a dream.

From the entrance hall, stairs curved upwards.
There were pot plants, on a plinth a sculpture of a
naked woman. In an illuminated alcove was a sculpted
head.

'It's you,' she exclaimed.

Lingering, she saw the head's bold shape, the
curving hairline, the intelligent brow. Her hand
tingled to touch it and the inner battle to prevent it
from doing so alarmed her. From what source, she
wondered, had the impulse come? It wasn't—it
couldn't have been affection, and it certainly was not
love.

'People either hate it or love it,' Evan said behind
her, making her jump. 'What does it do to you?'

'Nothing,' she answered quickly, then, as he turned
her, she saw the original and her pulses leapt. It's
because of what happened between us at the chalet,
she told herself, panicking.

He took hold of her chin while he scanned her face.
His smile was fleeting but full of secret knowledge, his
lips as they brushed hers were light and cool.

'Come,' he said, taking her hand and leading her to
the stairs. 'That head of me is the work of a sculptor
friend. One day, he'll model one of you.'

'No, thank you,' Fran answered frigidly, trying to
remove her hand from his. 'I may have become your
wife, but there's no need for me to join the Dowd
family's art gallery.' She had to climb quickly to keep
up with his strong strides.

They went from one room to another and Fran saw
a kaleidoscope of brown and gold, of yellow and rich
red. Reproduction furniture was teamed with cottage-
comfortable sofas and deep chairs. The circular dining

table was polished until the candles and table settings gleamed back their reflection. There were flowers and paintings and decorative plates displayed on the walls.

Fran was dazzled and overwhelmed, but the prevailing good taste made a deep impression on her. 'I admire your choice,' she commented, her hands clasped tightly at her waist. 'Or was it your wife's?'

'Ex-wife's,' he corrected. 'Don't make that mistake again. And no, it's mine. I bought this place two years ago. Willa never lived here.' He leaned back, arms folded, against a red upholstered dining chair. 'Are you glad about that?' His smile taunted. 'No other woman has lived here.' He added, eyes lazy, 'As a permanency.'

'I get your meaning.' Fran turned away.

Two seconds later, she was in the grip of arms so strong she could scarcely move. His face was a breath away. 'You know the ways of a man, do you? Well, know this, too. From now on, you share everything of mine, and I——' he held her away and raked her with a look of sharp desire, 'will share everything of yours.' His hand closed over a breast, while his mouth covered hers.

Against her conscious will, her body recalled the pleasure of his touch and she found herself delighting in the strange, new familiarity between them. Her arms crept round his neck and her lips started shyly to return his kisses.

When he lifted his head, she said with a small smile, 'Unlike you, I don't have any worldly goods.'

His gaze flashed over her animated features. 'This is enough.' His voice was deep. 'All I want from you is everything that you, as a woman, can give me.' Not as herself, she noted, but as a woman. He was speaking about her objectively. Well, that was what she wanted, wasn't it? He held her against him, his hands outspread around her rear. 'Do you understand now how you set me alight?'

She found herself asking, 'Only on a physical level?' then grew annoyed with herself for asking such a revealing question.

'Of course. It's what was agreed between us. And the reason we married.'

He ran his hands over her hair and pressed back her head so that her face tipped up. 'Never again, we decided, would either of us meet someone who would make no emotional demands on us. We're both of us free to come and free to go, provided, and this is paramount, our marriage remains intact.'

Fran surprised herself by shivering. His words had been almost as much a vow as those they had just made at the wedding ceremony. It was time, she decided, to state her case, to make some conditions of her own. 'No sharing of interest,' she declared. 'No coming together, causing emotional dependence.'

He did not contradict her. Had she, she asked herself, really expected him to do so? 'Most of all,' he took her up, 'no jealousy, since the marriage won't be threatened, no matter how many extra-marital affairs we each have.'

'No jealousy,' she echoed, suppressing from her inner vision a taunting image of his ex-wife then found that, for some strange reason, she wanted to hurt him. 'So you won't object if I go around with other men. Such as your stepbrother?'

His jaw moved aggressively and he detached himself from her. 'Ralph you will leave alone.' His eyes glittered. 'Understand?'

Fran turned aside. 'Now I know exactly why you married me—to keep me away from Ralph.'

'I'll tell you why I married you. A business man like me needs a wife, not just a succession of bed partners.

I've been looking for a long time for the right woman—one with a cool head and a cold heart. At the chalet I realised you could be that woman. I learnt enough about your character, your wish to avoid any emotional attachment——'

'The cold heart?' she broke in.

He nodded and continued, 'Your deliberate decision to meet Ralph there and put your relationship with him on a more intimate footing—'

'The cool head?'

He nodded again. 'I knew I'd be a fool to let you slip through my hands.'

I've changed since then, she thought, I've changed fundamentally. But how, and in what respect, she could not define.

'As you see,' he was speaking again, his mouthline hard, 'it was, on my part, a cold-blooded decision. Feelings did not enter into it.' He watched for her reaction, but her eyes on him did not falter. 'So you see, I needed you, in my own heartless way.'

Her gaze flickered then, but she took up his challenge. 'As a business partner and——' for a moment she could not hold his eyes, 'and a woman to sleep with.'

'Right, my darling.' His eyes were gleaming slits and she felt absurdly as though he had cut her flesh. A stride brought him to face her, a movement wound his arm round her waist, his mouth hitting hers closed her eyes and put a weakness into her legs. 'I'm not waiting,' he said, his voice muffled. 'I want you now.'

He was her husband, she couldn't refuse. *I don't want to refuse* ... She caught up with her own thoughts. It's my body remembering, not my emotions, she told herself. He was undressing her, kissing each exposed part, his lips hard on her excited flesh. He lifted her, leaving her clothing scattered where it had fallen and carried her upstairs.

A mixture of bright colours and floral patterns registered dimly on Fran's hazed vision and the coolness of the wide bed's covers hit her warmed skin. A few moments later, Evan's hard body was beside her, his fingertips trailing her nakedness, creating rising, insistent responses and bringing her arms up to his neck to hold him convulsively.

Yet he held away, resisting her pressure and laughing at her small frown of puzzlement. Then he relented and caressed her again with his hands and his lips, fastening his mouth over her hardened nipples until her body arched, inviting him . . .

'Oh, Evan, Evan,' she heard herself breathe as he came into her, 'I want——' What did she want, she wondered mistily, except this—this delight he was offering her? She responded to his urgency, giving pleasure for pleasure until, gasping, she reached with him a shared and sun-bright summit, lying afterwards, flesh throbbing, in the circle of his arms.

'It was good, so good,' she whispered.

'This time you wanted me,' he answered softly. 'Welcomed me and needed me.' His eyes held a gleam. 'And don't even try to deny it.'

Her brow pleated. 'I needed you?' She shook her head, her cheeks rubbing the muscle in his upper arm. 'That implies dependence, involvement.'

'Dreaded words,' he derided with a smile. Then his head found her pillow and his eyes closed. She looked down at him and a feeling welled and with it a faint panic. It's what's just happened, she assured herself, a man-and-woman closeness that arises from such a very special intimacy.

He stirred and she felt his desire returning. Low down, something in her began to respond. No, she thought, fighting her body's increasing need, no ... I don't want to become one with this man again. His hand rested with undisputed possession against her stomach, moving lower still.

'No,' she heard herself cry, 'I won't let you take control of me.'

She tried to tear from his arms. 'I won't become part of you, do you hear?'

He stayed motionless, holding her easily until her struggles tailed off. She found his eyes and her skin prickled at their coldness.

'It's the act of sex I'm after,' he said cuttingly, 'not the act of love. Now,' his hands tightened on her legs, tugging them, 'give me what I want.'

Drawing a ragged breath, she felt him take her. Against her will, she found her senses soaring, and when her pleasure reached its height, she gave a shuddering sigh and collapsed into him. He held her tightly beside him, still together, and finally they slept one against the other.

The door bell disturbed them, three long rings. It must have been a signal since Evan said, 'My father. Don't worry,' as Fran stiffened, 'he has a key.' He moved her from him and a sudden shivering made her shake inside. His leaving had left her empty and cold. 'He's an understanding person,' Evan assured her, 'when he wants to be.' He shouted, 'Get yourself a drink, Father. We'll be with you soon.'

There came an answering shout from the floor below and Evan rolled off the bed and stood up, stretching himself strongly. His smile, as he looked down on the wondering eyes and satiated form of his wife, held a taunt and a satisfaction that made her comment with a shy smile.

'If you were a cat, I'd say you'd just emptied a carton of cream.'

His lashes lowered and he answered, skimming over her with his look, 'If we were still alone, I'd lap up that cream all over again.' His hand reached out, but he checked it, then it caught her arm and pulled. 'Come, take a quick shower with me.'

He twisted her straight into his arms and, their laughter mingling, carried her through a door and under the shower.

Fifteen minutes later, he left her, saying over his shoulder, 'Five minutes. If you're any longer, I'll come and get you.'

On his way down the stairs, he burst into song. Hearing it, Fran held her breath. It was Johnny singing . . . Had it been Johnny Black who had made such passionate love to her?

CHAPTER FIVE

STANDING in the doorway, Fran paused. The tall, distinguished-looking man across the room was giving her a long, penetrating look. Just a little daunted, she gave him back his look, not boldly but with a deep interest. Sir Lionel Dowd was a respected figure, and not only throughout his own publishing empire. Much photographed, but rarely seen in person, his staff and employees, which numbered thousands, regarded him highly if also with awe.

It was with that awe, and some trepidation, that Fran looked at him now. He was her father-in-law! The fact almost made her sway. One after the other today, these small unnerving truths were exploding like bullets around her feet. She would have to make her way with care through the combined fire of those two very similar pairs of eyes.

The white-haired man approached, hand outstretched. Fran warmed to him at once, her uncertainty being overridden by a rush of gratitude at his unhesitating admission of her into his world.

'My son,' he said, holding her hand with both of his, 'appears to have made a wiser choice second time around. Evan should have invited his parents to his wedding, however simple the ceremony.'

Fran could only nod. She was overwhelmed by the man's directness and his approachability. He waited a moment, probably expecting her to speak, then went on encouragingly, 'I understand you're not only a member of the family, but also of the Dowd business empire?'

Fran answered his smile shyly and shook her head. 'Not really, Sir Lionel. A paid employee is a more accurate description.'

'And,' he threw over his shoulder, 'your wife is a pedant Evan, where words are concerned. Which, since words are our business, is an excellent attribute.' He released her hand. His wise eyes rested again on her face. 'My judgment tells me that you have a generous and loving nature, characteristics which my son's first wife most certainly did not possess.' He retrieved his drink and held it up. 'I offer a toast; Evan, Francesca—may your union be long-lasting and, most important, filled with a deep, two-way affection.'

His summing-up of her character, his conviction that her marriage to his son was based on love, made her panic. The net, she felt, was closing round her. She felt also that it was necessary to be honest with this kindly, sincere man. 'We married for expedience, Sir Lionel, nothing else.' In spite of his frown, she persisted, 'It was how I wanted it; and Evan, too. He'd had a painful experience with his first marriage, and I——'

'You've been married before?'

'No. It was my parents—they split up. After thirty years. It hit me hard, took away my belief that any relationship, even if initially it's based on love, can last.'

Sir Lionel invited her to sit down. Evan, who had been standing, indicated a three-seater settee. His upraised brows and serious expression told her it would be advisable to obey his directive, however much it went against the grain. Fran placed herself at its extreme end, but he chose to sit not at the other end as she had assumed, but beside her. His nearness, after their recent intimacy, made her skin prickle.

'Do you ever see your parents?' Evan's father asked from the depths of an armchair.

'No, they're not part of my life now.'

'Come, my dear,' Sir Lionel sat forward, hands clasped, 'that's a very bitter remark for a daughter to make. Can't you try to forgive?'

'How can I?' she asked, finding her palms were moist. 'I'm haunted by memories—of a happy childhood, by my parents' laughter and me between them holding their hands.' Fran tried a smile, but it evaded her. 'It's not the ghosts, it's the happy memories that do the damage. Stupid, isn't it?'

Evan rose and she felt as though something strong and secure had gone from her side.

Sir Lionel leaned back. 'I would have thought,' he said, 'that such things were to be cherished.'

Again, she shook her head. 'It's like having a cancelled-out childhood. By their action, my parents' have as good as asked me to forget about—well, things like the happiness we shared, the presents they gave me. And things like,' she searched for words, 'like the sparkling Christmas trees which they went out of their way to decorate just for me.'

A drink was placed in her hand. Gratefully, she looked up at Evan, but his face revealed cynicism and dismissal. 'Grow up, Francesca.' He dropped down to the settee, this time taking the other end. 'You've had the good things that many kids don't even know about. Be thankful for that.'

'Part of me is thankful,' she returned, 'the other parts feels so horribly let down. Which is why I decided,' she addressed her father-in-law, 'never to marry for love.'

His brows lifted. 'Am I to take it that although you've married my son, you don't love him.'

'He doesn't love me,' Fran blurted out in self-defence. 'Ask him. He told me he'd learned his lesson from his first marriage. He said he could offer me everything except love.' His brows had not descended so she turned pleadingly to Evan. 'Tell your father,' she urged, 'that what I'm saying is true. That you offered me marriage without affection——'

'And you accepted on those terms,' Evan broke in. 'Yes, it's true.'

Sir Lionel lifted himself from the chair and gazed down at his son and new daughter-in-law. 'You've made your marriage bed, both of you.' He shook his head as if deeply puzzled. 'The only advice I can give you is to lie on it and enjoy everything it has to offer. Make her happy there, son, otherwise, yours is going to be an empty relationship indeed.' He went to the door. 'I thought that, at my age, I'd heard everything, but this—arrangement beats the lot.'

He looked hard, first at his son, then at Fran. What he saw in her face she could not guess, but a smile broke into his seriousness and he seemed to leave a happier man.

'Will you take me home?' Fran asked, as the sound of Sir Lionel's car faded.

Evan's face held no readable expression. 'This is your home now,' he averred.

'Not—not yet. I have to adjust. If anyone had told me when I got up this morning that by evening I'd be a married woman, I'd have said they were crazy.' She attempted a smile. 'I'm beginning to think,' she put a hand to her head, 'that *I'm* crazy. It's all moved so quickly,' she repeated, 'please, Evan—will you try to understand?'

His open-necked shirt showed a patch of dark hair, and his jaw was shaded with faint, evening roughness. Her mind danced back to those gasping moments under the shower they had shared and she had forcibly to hold back an uprush of sensation. He can fire my desire, she panicked, with just a look!

At last, he said, 'I'll be away for the next few days. I'll give you that time to clear out your flat and give the landlord notice of your leaving. When I return, I'll arrange for your belongings to be collected and brought here.'

A sense of relief swamped her, like being let out of imprisonment from Evan's world and being allowed to go back to her own. 'Thank you,' she said smiling.

'There's no need to be so darned grateful,' Evan responded tartly. 'It gives the impression that you'll be glad to get away from me.'

I will . . . she heard the words in her mind, but for some reason they did not make it to her lips.

'I'll——' she motioned to the door, 'get my things.' He nodded, watching her go. She stopped and her eyes collided with his. 'Evan, I——' she twisted the rings which felt so strange on her finger, 'I'll be everything you want me to be as your wife——'

'Except loving. That's out.'

'Loving's out,' she answered, wondering why her lips trembled a little as she spoke.

He smiled, approaching slowly, eyes watching her. He stopped in front of her and she tensed, thinking he was going to reach out. He did, but not with his arms. She felt the impact of his physical power over her, felt her responses clamouring to be indulged, wanting him to touch her.

She turned and ran, dreading that he might follow, looking back at the turn of the stairs to see if he had.

He was in the hall looking up, laughter in his eyes as they mocked her retreat from him.

The days of Evan's absence sped by in a whirl of

packing and work. Fran had put away her rings. Her life, she felt, needed to pause and get its breath back. There would be plenty of time, she decided, to tell Judy, her deputy, and all the others about her change in status, both marital and social.

It was the change in the latter that most weighed on her mind. Once her colleagues knew of her marriage into the Dowd family, it would, she was sure, put a barrier between herself and the others, and that was the last thing she wanted. In any case, she mused, the whole incredible episode of meeting and then marrying Evan Dowd was becoming like a dream, even to herself.

When the telephone rang in her two-bedroomed apartment, it was Friday evening. Her arm jerked as it reached out to silence the bell. It just had to be Evan. No one else would ring her . . .

She had forgotten Ralph! 'How nice to hear from you,' she mouthed the platitude thinking furiously, What am I going to tell him?

'Fran, I'm just back from Germany. The family told me, my mother, my stepfather. But I don't believe it's true. They were just trying to keep me away from you.'

'Ralph, I——' She pushed her fingers into the thickness of her hair. 'I have to talk to you. You know where I live. I'm still here, at the flat.'

'This evening? At seven?'

Ralph's voice was so eager, Fran could have cried. 'Seven,' she agreed. 'And Ralph, I have to tell you—it's true.' Her hand shook a little as she replaced the receiver.

He was on time, grey eyes filled with appeal, mouth curved in an I-know-you-were-joking smile. He took her hands and scanned them. 'No rings. I knew they were fooling me.' The relief on his face nearly broke Fran's heart.

He pulled her towards him but at the last moment, she managed to turn her head and his mouth pressed into her cheek. 'I was so angry, Fran,' he said, 'when I knew I wouldn't be able to join you at the chalet, you don't know how angry. Then to know you were caught there at Evan's mercy—since his wife left him, he's been quite unscrupulous with women. I wanted to warn you, but he wouldn't let me.'

Fran's lids lowered, hiding her trepidation at the revealing statement. He thought it was with relief at his return and put his arms round her. She stiffened and he said, 'If only I'd told you my real feelings for you——'

'Don't.' Her hand covered his mouth. Evan had said to him on the 'phone at the chalet, Yes, I'll tell her how much you love her . . . He caught at her hand as it touched his mouth, but she removed it gently.

'You should have told me, Ralph,' she answered urgently. 'If I'd known, I'd never have agreed to meet you in Switzerland.'

'You think I didn't know that? I arranged to meet you there with the intention of spending the weekend making love to you. I was sure that by then I'd have undermined your barriers so much you'd have agreed to marry me.'

'Ralph,' Fran said, desperation tightening her throat, 'you know I wouldn't have let things get that far.'

'I'm certain I'd have made you change your mind.' A little of her despair had entered into him. 'I was afraid to tell you outright about my feelings,' he insisted. 'I thought that after we'd made love you'd have started loving me back.'

'Oh, Ralph,' she shook her head and pulled away from him.

'It's not too late,' he said, eyes bright with hope.

'We're here, alone.' He looked around, but Fran knew he was not even seeing the chaos, the filled boxes, the overflowing cases. He saw the bedroom through an open door and started to urge her that way. 'Fran, please——' He tightened his arms and straightened her against him. 'At least let me kiss you. I've never kissed you properly. I put up with all that hand-holding knowing that one day I'd persuade you to let me go all the way.'

He found her mouth and pressed his own against it. She did not have the heart to push him away. He stopped to get his breath and she knew she had to tell him the truth.

'Ralph,' she said, 'it *is* true what your parents told you. I did m——'

The door opened and Evan stood there, eyes glittering with a cold fire.

Ralph's arms dropped away and Fran was left standing alone. Evan strolled in but his relaxed manner was at odds with the searing condemnation in his face.

'I see you've taken me at my word,' he clipped. 'Four days into our marriage and you've taken on a lover.'

'So you are married.' Ralph's voice was choked. 'But you're wrong, Evan. We hadn't quite got that far.' His stare converged with Evan's on Fran's face. 'Thank goodness,' he added. 'If I'd known when I came what a dirty trick she'd played on me, I wouldn't have touched her.'

Fran hid her surprise at seeing this new side of Ralph. 'You did know,' she defended herself. 'Your parents had told you, and so had I, but you chose not to believe us. And what dirty trick did I play on you? I told you at the start of our friendship that I couldn't ever offer emotion or love in any relationship.'

'So you married Evan without love. I don't believe you.'

'You see,' Fran exclaimed, 'you're doing it again— not believing. Yes, we——' she wondered why she had hesitated, 'we married without loving each other. Ask Evan.'

'Ask the lady,' Evan flipped back as Ralph appealed to him. He watched his stepbrother's expression change to one of renewed hope. 'But,' he took a step in Ralph's direction, 'if I catch you with your arms round my wife again, I'll——'

'Don't threaten him, please,' Fran broke in, 'I'd never set brother against brother.'

'You've done that already,' Ralph said, and the hurt in his eyes made Fran want to reach out in pity.

After he had gone, there was a brief, breath-holding silence. Which way would Evan jump? Fran panicked. He must have seen the fear since he laughed, but it was a sound that grated.

Slowly he approached, binding his arms round her waist and pulling her to him. 'Now I know what has turned up on my doorstep in the form of a wife,' he said, eyes glinting like light on a diamond. Fran's pride recoiled at the deliberate insult. 'Now I know what a predatory woman I've taken unto myself. I was the first to awaken her desires and I appear to have turned her overnight into a near-nymphomaniac.' The glint of a diamond turned into that of a flashing sword.

'So you couldn't wait,' he said between clenched jaws. 'You had to try to get a man into your bed, and one I had expressly told you to leave alone—my very vulnerable stepbrother. So,' his arm muscles hardened and he swung her up, 'I'll give you what my unexpected return seems to have prevented your enjoying. But, my love,' his hard lips grazed her ear, 'I'll give it so much better than my under-experienced brother.'

'Evan,' Fran protested, trying to escape but knowing it was useless, 'it's not like you think it is. I was going to tell him the truth. That's why I invited him here.'

'There's the telephone,' he pointed out grimly and set her down in the bedroom, tugging her cotton sweater over her head. Her hair loosened from its topknot and tumbled over her shoulders.

'Do you think I didn't try telling him that way?' she defended herself, clawing back her hair from her eyes. Then she felt chilled and looked down. He was removing her final barrier, lifting her and discarding it.

Unexpectedly, he stopped, his mouth a slash of curving red. 'Now undress me.' His hands went to his hips and he seemed turned to granite as she tensed at his command. 'We're not moving from this spot until you do,' he added, his tone dangerously soft.

She moistened her lips with the point of her tongue. Her hands lifted and dropped. 'I've never——'

'Then learn.'

This man, she thought, this man's been my lover, I've taken him to me more intimately than any other human being. Yet I don't know him, he's like a stranger . . . Her heart pounded as she went for his shirt buttons, peeling the garment from the width of his shoulders, and sliding it over unhelpful arms.

His waist was taut as she loosened his belt, unfastened his waistband—then stopped at the more familiar act required of her. 'Please pull that zip,' she whispered, shyly seeking his eyes. He did not move. She reached out and slowly slid the fastener.

He grew impatient at her slowness and completed

the job then, as naked as she was, he jerked her to his hard demanding body.

A wave of longing washed over her and her head went back. Her hair hung down and he gathered it into one hand, pulling it to move her head one way and then the other. Her lips parted in a pleasure-gasp and his came down, drinking a kiss from her mouth and urging her backwards on to the bed.

He joined her without breaking the kiss and the impact of his weight on her made her moan. He had done nothing to ease the fall. His hands were stroking and seeking vulnerable places, bringing her to a pitch of desire that caused her breaths to shorten and quicken.

Her hands around his head moved involuntarily to pull him even closer and when he linked with her he was rough with a thrusting need. At the height of their pleasure he was both giving and taking and she drew her breaths from her depths, calling his name and murmuring words she could not hear for the clamour of her pulses.

Then it was over and she was exclaiming, 'Oh, Evan, Evan, I hope—I wish—I want——' But there was a strange embargo on every expression of delight and she finally hid her face against the roughness of his chest and lay against him in a golden glow.

It was not sleep that claimed her but a deep contentment that, after a while, lifted her eyelids dreamily. Her slumbrous eyes found Evan's and her lips curved into a smile. He was looking down at her, resting on his elbow, but there was no smiling response to her silent statement of happiness. She remembered the time he had first made love to her. The aftermath, she recalled, had been a little like this, making her wonder whether he dismissed so coldly every woman he had made love to. Now she was beginning to know his ways. When he had taken all he wanted, he drew back into his remote and distant self.

Which was what he had meant when he had told her he needed her in his own *heartless* way. What she couldn't understand was why the discovery should upset her so much. Her 'no involvement' vow should have enabled her to repay him in his own coin—turn away from him, take her clothes and leave him, as if all she, too, had wanted was the satisfaction of her own desires.

But could she, she wondered, imitate him and shrug off that wonderful thing that had happened to her while she was in Evan's arms? Could a woman make love without loving, as a man could? To her infinite sorrow, she was, in her own case, beginning to learn the answer.

'For the past few days,' Fran heard him say as he swung from the bed, 'I've been in Amsterdam.' He had pulled on his shirt and partly buttoned it. 'On business. I met Willa there.' As Fran's head shot round, his eyebrows lifted sardonically. 'On business.'

Plucking at the bedcover, Fran pulled it over her. 'Yet you stand in judgment on me for what you imagine I've done in your absence?'

'I repeat,' he replied coldly, 'on business. She needs work. She's had her troubles and has got out of the modelling mainstream.' He was beside the bed, looking down at the flushed, frowning face. 'I want you to give her a job.'

Fran swung her legs to the floor, winding the cover around her. 'If she means so much to you,' she retaliated, 'why didn't you take her back as your wife?' The wonderful feeling had quite gone and she wanted to hit out at the man who had given it to her, yet seen fit to snatch it away.

He ignored her outburst. 'Until her circumstances

altered,' he went on, 'she was earning high fees. She's an accomplished model and knows the art backwards.'

'I'm sorry,' Fran fluffed out her hair, pretending nonchalance, then she caught his look and saw that she had unconsciously been provocative, 'but, as I told you in Switzerland, her style isn't that of the magazine.'

He tugged away her covering and seized her by the shoulders, looking her over with lust in his gaze. 'If you make sexy gestures, then follow them with a challenge, you'll get what you're asking for.' He pushed her back and the bed springs groaned under their combined weight. This time she fought him with her strength and her words. 'I hate you, Evan Dowd,' she said, her voice low, 'you're callous and you're cold and you're tricking me with your personality all the time.'

He lifted himself and looked at her. 'Hate me,' he replied, his mouth curved in a travesty of a smile, 'it matters that much to me.' And he clicked his fingers in her face. He smiled as she flinched. 'If your lover turns into your boss on the marriage bed, it's just too bad. But I'm repeating,' his eyes changed and Fran found her lips parting in anticipation, 'give Willa a job. She'll cope.' Then all her powers of resistance were overcome by his long, drugging kiss.

When it was over, Evan stood up. Fran was left wanting, expecting more. He saw this and smiled. 'Where's the shower in this chaotic apartment?'

'There isn't one, just a bath,' she returned, dragging herself upright and trying to calm her throbbing heart. 'This is how the other half live.' She dared the light in his eyes, knowing that she had challenged him again. 'You go first.' His hand came out but she evaded it. 'It isn't large enough for two.'

He shrugged and followed her directions. As she sat waiting, sheet around her sarong-style, the singing came, the song he—no, Johnny Black—had sung that day at the chalet. She held her head, sure she was imagining; covered her ears, clenched her fists.

He emerged to find her locked inside herself. He was smiling, eyes mocking, the man called Johnny was reaching out. It was impossible to hold back, and as she felt his arms close around her, her head drooped to rest on his shoulder and it was like catching a glimpse of sunlight after a wild storm.

He kissed her and it was tenderness itself this time. Almost as if there was love between them, except that his slanting smile told a story of elusiveness and no commitment. What he said was out of the blue. 'We're going to Germany, you and I,' he smiled. 'A kind of honeymoon. Tomorrow afternoon, after you've vacated this flat.'

Drawing sharply from him, she tightened the sheet around her underarms. 'Evan, I can't. I have work to do, photographic sessions to arrange, modelling agencies to contact, plus the necessary trips abroad for background.'

'I'll take you to those. The Rhine, ancient castles, picturesque places. And I've told you the model's name—Willa Hemming.'

'Once Willa Dowd,' Fran flashed back. 'You still have feeling for her, maybe even love her, so you're doing her a good turn. You're instructing one of your minions—myself—to take her on, regardless of her suitability—or even her ability to do the job required of her.'

The blue of his eyes had deepened. 'Don't denigrate the woman. She's adaptable and even malleable. She'll do what you want of her.'

There was pain in the region of Fran's heart that drove her on. 'And you should know, shouldn't you? She's been your mistress, your wife and now your mis——' She let out a cry. A relentless grip had jerked her round, another had grasped a bunch of her disordered hair.

'That statement you'll withdraw,' his face was cold and dangerous, 'or I'll make you wish you'd never been born.'

How could he speak to her so, she cried inside, and all in defence of the woman who, he alleged, had made him forswear love until his life ended?

He was hurting her so much, she felt herself go pale. 'I'm sorry,' she whispered, and covered her face when he let her go.

'Now get your bath. In the morning, I'll hire a firm to collect this stuff. When you're ready, we'll go home.'

'Home', she thought, locking herself in the bathroom, is alleged to be where the heart is. By that reckoning, Evan's home can never be mine, because my heart isn't his, and never will be. Will it?

CHAPTER SIX

FRAN pushed open the balcony doors and stepped outside. The view flung away into the distance and she leant against the rails and gazed around.

'There,' Evan pointed, coming to stand beside her, 'is the Odenwald, forest and hills and footpaths. And there,' his arm moved, 'are the hills beyond the Rhine. On a clear day, it's possible to see as far as the Taunus mountains, north of Frankfurt. And there,' his arm lifted, 'are the vineyards on the west bank of the Rhine.'

Fran exclaimed, 'It's wonderful, Evan.' She looked down at the cultivated lawns and footpaths between the apartment blocks, where people walked; she saw the children's play area and laughed at the rabbits that chased each other across the grass.

Turning, she entered the lounge and took a second look around her. Here, she perceived another aspect of Evan's taste. The wall paintings were modern, mere slashes of colour, their asymmetrical patterns emitting sharp wordless messages. The furniture was made of steel and glass; the carpet pattern geometrical in black and white.

'Stunning,' Fran commented.

'You haven't asked me, as most of my visitors do, whether I chose this stuff when I had a hangover.'

Fran laughed, pushing back her hair which she had left loose. 'I like the feel of the place. It appeals to my instinct for colour boldness.'

'You don't find it stark?'

'No, no.' She looked around again. 'I find it exciting.'

He looked at her again, his eyelids lowered reflectively. 'You intrigue me,' he said. 'One by one, you're lowering the veils over your personality.'

Fran coloured, shaking her head. 'After the seventh, there's nothing,' she told him. 'Just a piece of ice. I did warn you.'

'Ah, but,' he approached, 'your ice to my fire—what a combination. You melt in my arms.'

Fran stepped back, agitatedly, clutching her suitcases. Evan smiled at her evasive action, taking them from her, and leading the way to the bedroom. 'There are three,' he explained, 'each with *en suite* facilities.'

'Good. I'll know there's somewhere for me to go if we quarrel.'

He smiled, head slightly down, threatening vengeance. Fran avoided his eyes because his present mood affected her so powerfully. That side of him—it appeared now and then, the human side, the *Johnny* side. It was elusive and tantalising and it did something to her she couldn't identify.

The colour scheme in the bedroom was grey and white and Fran found it curiously pleasing. Here and there were brightly floral touches, in the curtains and the bedroom chair covers.

'You like?' Evan asked, leaning sideways against the door.

'I like,' she replied, smiling.

'Good.' He straightened. 'The bedroom plays an important part in a marriage.' He came towards her. 'At this moment, there's something very feminine about you I can't resist.' His arms went round her and his eyes dropped to rest on the swell of her breasts. 'I want you, Francesca. Last night I restrained my urges at your request. Now, I want to renew my acquaintance with you.'

His kiss was long and compelling and Fran resisted

its soft persuasion. 'I'm tired from the flight, Evan,'
she said, cheek against his shoulder. 'And the
journey from the airport.' She looked around. 'And
the newness.' He let her go, going from the room.
She looked after him, finding inside herself relief
tinged with a paradoxical disappointment. He must,
she thought, have some kind of feeling for me,
otherwise, he would have forced himself on me . . .
Last night he'd been considerate, and now also. Her
heart went out to him in a swirl of gratitude, then
she clawed it back, because on no account, she told
herself, must she lose control of that organ in her
body.

Later, they sat on the balcony in the sunshine of
the spring evening. Fran lay back, eyes closed,
holding her drink. Evan was renewing his and she
was momentarily alone. The sound of the traffic was
distant, peoples' voices rose from below, amplified
by the apartment blocks around them, but Fran
knew so little of their language she could not
understand what they said. That, in itself, she found
calming.

She had only to open her eyes and the view was
there, pleasing her mind and her sight. There was a
movement in the balcony doorway. Involuntarily, she
looked up and her pulses leapt at the narrow, male
stare. Time moved on and Evan resumed his seat,
leaning back.

Her heart pounded as if she had just avoided a head-
on crash. It worried her that she should feel this way
and she tried to find the reason why. It's being newly-
married, she concluded, having a man of my own
around for the first time in my life.

When Evan spoke, she jumped, her glass spilling.
He made no attempt to help, just watched as she
dabbed at her skirt. Then he spoke again. 'Have you

arranged any appointments for fashion shots while you're here?'

She shook her head. 'I was waiting for you to suggest locations.'

He nodded, drank, then enquired, 'Booked any models to come over?'

'Not yet. I need to have a venue, give a time, tell Judy, my assistant, the type of outfits I want sent over.'

He nodded again seeming satisfied.

'And,' she added, giving him a testing sideways glance, 'the type of girl needed to wear the clothes.'

He nodded once more, but the view held his eyes. Good, thought Fran, he isn't pressing the point about his ex-wife, which must mean he'd dropped the idea. Involuntarily, she sighed and a coil of tension unwound inside her, tension which, until that moment, she did not even realise was there.

'This evening,' Evan said to the view, 'I have a dinner engagement.'

Her head swung towards him. The tension was back, coiling round her insides. 'You said this was to be a honeymoon,' she half-accused.

'I believe I said a kind of honeymoon?' he corrected, eyebrows raised. 'Fitted in between my business engagements. Did I forget to mention it?'

Her spirits dived like a shot bird and her pleasure died with them. 'I wish you had told me.'

He got up, bending over the back of her chair. 'Why, does it make a difference?'

'No, no, of course not. It's just that——' What was it? she asked herself, because it had made a difference. 'Just that——' her smile shone falsely, 'I like to know in advance about such things and——'

He was pulling her to her feet. 'Stop babbling nonsense,' he mouthed against her lips, 'and admit

you're disappointed. You're getting to like my kind of
loving and you were anticipating an evening in my
arms.'

'I was not!' She twisted to avoid his mouth but he
pinned it down, invaded it and exchanged her taste
with his. When he had finished, she could only look
up at him, bright-eyed and at a loss for words.

'Now,' he said, 'go into that bedroom and get
yourself ready to be taken out.' He pulled her upright.

'I'm going with you?'

'Did you really think I'd leave you behind?' He
looked her over, appreciating her gold-coloured dress.
'Don't change. What you're wearing is right. You've a
sophisticate's body but,' his lips trailed hers, 'the face
of an innocent. A tantalising mix.' His eyes crinkled at
the corners and his smile was fleetingly warm.

'Evan, I——'

'Yes?' The eyes, like the tone, had cooled. He
released her.

'Nothing.' She hurried to the bedroom, standing in
the centre of the room and putting her fingers to her
temples. Had Evan guessed what her lips and tongue
had connived to say and almost succeeded? Taking her
unawares and telling a lie? For she didn't love him,
she did not! It was neither possible nor allowable.

It was everything he represented that she loved—
status, security; his companionship, his admiration
that made her feel good; and, she could not deny it, his
physique and his virility. Those were material, surface
things, which did not involve emotion or depth of
feeling.

Comforted by her own reasoning, Fran restyled her
hair and renewed her make-up. From a cupboard she
took a matching jacket, changed her sandals for
slimline shoes and appraised her reflection. She sought
the detached determined woman she was convinced

she had become, only to discover that her fingers were twirling the rings Evan had given her in a gesture of uncertainty.

As they drove towards the town a few miles distant, Evan explained what the meeting involved. 'It's exploratory, a possible takeover by Dowd Wideworld of the family-run Müller magazine group. We're widening our publishing horizons,' he told her, 'not only here in Europe, but in other parts of the world.'

'Is all this a family secret?' Fran asked, face averted.

'You mean the Dowd family? No,' he corrected, 'it's the secret of the Dowd Wideworld board of directors.'

Fran nodded. 'Thanks for trusting me enough to tell me.'

'You're my wife,' he answered, and she wondered why the straightforward statement affected her so much.

She stared through the window at the slowly darkening, unfamiliar landscape. In the distance were wooded hills, while nearer, the fields crept almost to the roadside. Then the scenery changed into an urban area, where there were four- or five-storeyed houses with deep, pointed gables. The streets were wide and tree-lined with trams humming busily along one side.

The restaurant doors swung wide and one of a group of men turned their way. Recognition of Evan seemed to be instantaneous and a man approached, smiling, followed by his two companions.

It was then, Fran noticed, that Evan the business man, top executive, emerged like a blade from a penknife. This aspect of his personality, honed to sharpness, she had never seen before.

There was so much to learn—the thought cut through her mind—about the man who was, incredibly, her husband; so many sides of him to startle her, to torment and to dazzle. Would this angle of his

character, when the evening's business was over, settle
back into invisibility as the side of him called Johnny
had done?

He was conversing in fluent German, shaking hands
all round. He listened, smiling, and nodded, glancing
over his shoulder without apparently seeing the object
for which he looked. Then he brought Fran into the
group.

'My wife, Francesca,' he said, 'Fran, this is *Herr*
Helmut Müller,' a warm, strong hand engulfed Fran's,
'his son, Karl,' another firm handshake, 'and Dietmar,
his grandson.' The slim young man retained her hand
a fraction longer than necessary while she smiled up
into his eager face.

Helmut, white-haired, round-faced, said, 'It is my
great pleasure to meet you, *Frau* Dowd. You do not
know how pleased I am to hear that this young man,'
he nodded to Evan, 'has found himself the wife he has
been searching for. You see,' at her surprised smile, 'I
have known him for some little time now and
whenever I asked him, When are you marrying? he has
told me, When I find the perfect woman. So you see
you must be perfection.'

Fran joined in the laughter, but shook her head.
'There's a lot wrong with me. I'm——'

'Darling,' Evan's arm slid round her waist, 'why
spoil their illusions? I assure you, you fit my every
requirement.' He looked down into her wide gaze and
bent to whisper, 'Come, Fran, play our "perfect
lovers" game.'

Taking her cue, she put her hand into his, clasping it.
The pressure that came in return caused a pain to shoot
up her arm, but her smile did not waver. Instead, she
clenched her teeth secretly and when Evan led the way to
the table which, *Herr* Müller explained, had been held
for them, she followed without a word of protest.

The men stood waiting for Fran to take her seat. She acknowledged their politeness with a smile and did so, expecting them to join her at the table. Instead, the eyes of all four men were focused on a woman who approached across the restaurant. Was this, Fran wondered, the person for whom Evan had been looking?

She was tall and fair and slender and, give or take a feature or two, she might have been Willa Hemming's mirror image. By the way Evan's eyes rested on her, it seemed to Fran that he thought so, too. He likes her, Fran thought, feeling her insides curl like leaves crisping in autumn. Just look at his eyes—*he more than likes her*.

If she's his woman type, she thought, trying to solve the riddle, why did he marry me? But isn't it plain, she reasoned, why he chose for a wife someone as dissimilar as I am from his true taste? He'll be in no danger of falling in love with me, whereas he could fall devastatingly for the woman of his fantasies, which I definitely am not. Anyway, she chided herself, why should it matter that he picked me, whom he'll never love, as his legal partner? I only agreed to marry him because I knew I could never love him. Didn't I?

There was no chance to answer her own question because Evan seemed suddenly to have remembered her existence. 'Fran,' he said, 'this is *Fraulein* Richter, financial adviser to the Müller magazine group. Sabina, my wife, Francesca.'

He had called the woman by her first name!

'Your wife?' The warm, brown eyes widened, the beautiful face was lit with an apparently genuine pleasure. 'You have married at last?'

Her words, when coupled with those of *Herr* Müller, were surprising. Did none of these people know, she wondered, of Evan's first marriage? Or had it been so brief, Evan had thought it not worth mentioning?

The woman called Sabina was pressing her hand. 'I hope,' she was saying, 'you will both be very happy. Evan,' she spoke his name charmingly, 'maybe you will not want to work all those long, dark hours now?'

He smiled at the speaker, and Fran wondered acidly how many other secrets they shared.

Sabina seemed to have been allocated the seat next to Evan's, while Helmut Müller took his place on Evan's other side. Fran found herself between Dietmar, Helmut's grandson, and his father, Karl.

Dietmar was fair-haired and good-looking and Fran guessed him to be only a year or two older than herself.

He withdrew his eyes from the woman called Sabina, clasped his hands over the place setting and smiled. 'You will not be too bored, I hope, with the talk this evening?'

'Even if my mind wanders,' Fran answered with a smile and looking about her, 'all this is so new to me I'll be busy thinking about that.'

High on the restaurant's walls were deers' antlers and displays of patterned plates. Here and there, at different heights, were barrel ends bearing brewers' logos. The seats and tables were wooden, with cushions for comfort. In a central place on the table was a small flowering plant. The place-mats were a glowing red, setting off the sparkle of the cutlery.

'Have you accompanied your husband on many of his journeys overseas?' Dietmar was asking.

'This is the first,' Fran answered, 'we haven't been married very long.'

'Ah.' His right fist hit his left palm. 'To think I missed you by such a short time!' He laughed snapping his fingers in mock annoyance, making her laugh. Then her eyes were drawn to Evan, but all his attention was on the woman beside him. Every word she said seemed to be of tremendous importance to him. It was this shared seriousness that sparked off inside her a feeling of grievance she was not even aware she was nursing.

She found herself wanting to keep Dietmar's attention, not only because he was a pleasant person, but also as a kind of antidote to Evan's banishment of her from his mind.

'Evan's world of publishing, especially magazines—is really quite familiar to me,' she told him. 'I work on one of the Dowd publications.' She found a card in her handbag and gave it to Dietmar.

'Fran Williams,' he read out, 'fashion editor, *Woman's Choice.* So,' he gave her a long look, 'you are one of those frightening creatures, a lady journalist.'

'Very specialised,' she countered. 'I keep strictly to my own line.'

He nodded. 'Would you like this back? No? Good. I will keep it, then. See, I am putting it into my wallet which is not so far from my heart.'

He watched her laughter. Strangely, the light in his eyes dimmed and they swung along the table, seeking out Sabina's profile. Either he was trying to lip read, Fran decided, and get in on the conversation, or the fair-haired young woman who seemed to be fascinating her listeners—particularly Evan—had at some time hurt him badly.

As the evening progressed, Fran decided that it was the former, since Dietmar seemed to put himself out to give her the attention which Evan did not. He drew her into the discussion, and asked for her professional opinion, listening courteously as she gave it. And all the while, Evan's attentiveness to Sabina Richter did not waver.

The journey back to Evan's apartment was in a silence that crackled. That curious sense of grievance had not left her. It had threaded itself through the rest of the evening, tightening around her thoughts until her head ached with it.

Dropping her jacket on to a chair, she swung round to confront him. But with what? she asked herself, staring at him. With ignoring her and giving his attention and his admiration to another woman?

He had removed his tie and loosened the neck of his shirt. His tall body seemed relaxed, which gave his words, when he spoke them, so much more hurting power.

'I took you with me tonight to get your views about a possible takeover, not to conduct a blatant seduction of the youngest member of the Müller magazine group.'

'My opinion?' she exclaimed, reeling inwardly as if Evan had delivered a physical blow. 'When did you once ask me what I thought? Halfway through the discussion, you all switched to German. You know I don't understand a word of it.' Except, a tormenting voice whispered, *Ich liebe dich*—which I don't, I don't!

'You had a tame interpreter beside you,' Evan said. 'I saw Müller junior translating at regular intervals. All in all,' his hands slid into his pockets, 'he seemed to be very taken with you.' His lids lowered and his eyes did a sensual survey of her figure. 'There's no denying you have a lot to offer, but——' a couple of strides brought him to her, his hands curling round her forearms, 'you don't offer it to *him*. Do you understand?'

She tensed under his painful hold. 'So our so-called marriage is going to be all one-sided, is it?' she challenged. 'You can flaunt your admiration for other women as much as you like——'

'What other women?'

'*Fraulein* Richter, but,' she went on, 'on no account must I show any liking I might feel for another man.'

'Sabina Richter?' His eyes took on a reflective expression. He let her go. 'Mmm, Sabina's certainly something.'

Fran rubbed her arms, sure he had bruised her. 'All those "long dark hours" *Fraulein* Richter said you worked,' she tossed at him, 'how many of those did you and she spend together?'

He went slowly towards her, head slightly down. 'I've got myself a jealous wife, have I?' He didn't touch her but his eyes were tearing her to pieces. 'No love to give but possessive of the man she regards as legally hers.'

'I have as much right to make a comment about your—your dealings with Miss Richter as you had to make unpleasant innuendoes about myself and Dietmar Müller.'

'My dealings with Miss Richter were entirely of a business nature, which yours with Dietmar were patently not. I saw the way he looked at you.'

'And I,' she accused, 'saw the way you looked at Sabina.'

His jaw firmed, his hand wrapped around her waist. 'We're back to possessiveness, are we?' He jerked her against him. 'It's time I possessed you. That should wipe the jealousy from your mind.' He forced up her chin and scanned her features, putting his lips to her frowning brows. 'Hours have passed,' he murmured, 'since I had the feel of you against my flesh,' he breathed against her neck, 'inhaled the scent of you,' his hands covered a firming breast, 'felt you responding to my touch.'

There were sensations arising inside her, sensations that had been growing more familiar as the days had gone by. Every time Evan came near they manifested themselves—in a curious weakness in her legs, in hurried breathing, in an overwhelming desire to reach out and touch him. These were all completely natural, she assured herself hurriedly, all arising from a sexuality that had nothing whatsoever to do with the emotions.

He pulled her to him so that her forehead was against his chest. His hand reached round to pull down the fastener of her dress. In another moment, it was a pile of bright gold at her feet and there was little else in the way of clothing for him to deal with.

'I'll look at you,' he said, eyes desire-bright, 'as you say I looked at Sabina. Will that please you? Calm your jealousy, maybe?' Her breasts were throbbing now as his hand and his gaze aroused them to a pouting fullness. Then he bent down and put his mouth where his hand had been.

Her head went back and she found his shoulder, holding on to it for support.

'I'm not waiting any longer,' he said huskily. 'I want you now.' He lifted her, swinging her round and striding through the door to his bedroom.

The bed gave beneath her and in a few swift movements he shed his clothes. He lifted her again, his arms bringing her against his abrasive chest hair, his hard, expanding ribs. Her arms had wrapped themselves around him and their eyes interlocked, the brightness in hers merging with the fire in his.

'Say you want me,' he ordered gruffly, 'say you want me above all other men.'

She ran her tongue over her lips. It was true what he had said, she knew that, but it was a confession she wanted under no circumstances to make to him. She shook her head, burying her burning face in his shoulder.

'Say it,' he commanded, his hold about her body tightening, 'or I'll——'

'Above all other men,' she gasped, 'I want you. Oh Evan, I want you so much ...'

'Then, Francesca, you shall have me, not there but here,' he mouthed against her lips. He lifted her and lowered her to the carpet.

The surface was unyielding beneath her back and he came over her, his muscle-hard body as unforgiving as the floor's hardness. In a swift movement, he went into her, and the rhythmic movements had her crying out with pleasure and gasping his name as fulfilment broke through like the sun at dawn.

Hours later she awoke to find him leaning over her. He flicked her lips with a careless finger and smiled in such an intimate way her heart turned over. 'If you're as magnificent as that without love,' he said, 'what I wonder are you like with it?'

'You'll never know the answer,' she told him and watched his smile die. A shiver took hold at the look in his hard, cold eyes. It was at that moment that she knew the answer and it was one that shook her whole world.

Against her better judgment, despite all the promises she had made to herself, all her vows to remain emotionally frozen even though her body might have been burning up with desire—she had fallen in love with the man she had married!

The spring sunshine warmed the balcony on which she stood next morning, leaning against the parapet and gazing at the wide-sweeping view. But she did not really see its beauty. Her mind was staring inwards, trying to sort out the pieces into which her world had been shattered. She still had not recovered from the explosive effect of the knowledge which, in the warm, waking hours after the lovemaking, had come to her.

I don't love him, she tried to convince herself—it's the after-effect of our intimacy, the sense of closeness still lingering. She sighed, watching people going about their business below in the park-like surroundings of the apartment blocks.

It was useless trying to deny it—that feeling which had been growing of wanting to touch him, please him, of missing him when he was away. It explained, she realised, that sense of grievance she had experienced at seeing his attention to Sabina Richter and which had finally turned into a searing pain. It truly had been jealousy of the bitterest kind.

Rabbits jumped around the grass and burrowed in the sandpits in the children's play area. She wished she could follow their example and hide away from the incredible truth that had hit her only a few hours before.

The burst of a song over the hiss of the shower wafted out from inside the apartment. *When a woman lies beside a man* . . . Her heart somersaulted. It was the man called Johnny Black . . . He was the man she loved, she told herself feverishly, not Evan Dowd, hard-faced chief executive of Dowd Wideworld, but laughing, carefree Johnny Black. And, she told herself in a rush of strange reasoning, since that man called Johnny did not exist, therefore her love for him did not exist.

An arm hooked around her neck from behind and pulled her against a wet, strong body. 'I'm lonely in the shower,' a deep vibrating voice declared. 'Come, share it with me, woman.'

Damp hands turned her and she gazed, head back, into a bristle-shadowed, faintly devilish face and her heart spun in a crazy dance. How could she hide her feelings from this man? How to prevent him from learning her secret?

She smiled up at him without discovering the answer. 'Are you speaking now as my boss or my husband?' she asked.

Dark eyes under damp lashes flickered. 'Both,' he stated, swinging her into his arms.

She closed her eyes on the uprush of happiness and her mind to the consequences of her heart's folly.

Breakfast behind them, Evan said, 'The next few days are ours.'

A plan came to her to give her cover if her eyes should give away her feelings.

'Shall we,' she removed the tea towel she had tied around her waist to act as an apron, 'pretend we're lovers.' She dared not raise her eyes.

'We are.'

'I—I meant——' would he laugh at her suggestion? 'Make-believe we're——' dared she say it? '—we're in love?'

He did not answer.

'After all——' Was she pleading too hard, she wondered? '—this is a kind of honeymoon, isn't it? That's what you called it when you told me we were coming here.'

He still did not answer and she filled in the painful pause by pulling out drawers to discover where to put the clean cutlery. She frowned, a tight pain forming in her chest. 'If it's going to be impossible for you even to pretend we're in love, then forget it.'

Again she was manhandled from behind, this time by fingers which bit into her shoulders, turning her. He studied her expression, his own unreadable. The pain he was inflicting registered on her face, and it

seemed that this effectively masked those secret
feelings she was trying so desperately to hide.

He seemed to relax, the lines of his face softening
into a smile which temporarily assuaged Fran's dread
of her secret's discovery. But it told her without a
trace of a doubt how swiftly he would end their
relationship if she ever betrayed to him that she had
destroyed the whole basis of their marriage—that it
would be entirely loveless.

'It wouldn't be impossible,' he answered her softly,
holding her away to study her better, the smile giving
place to a hardened line, 'provided the pretence ends
just as soon as the few days of so-called honeymoon
are over.'

Wordlessly, she nodded. She could ask for no more
and she recognised yet again the terrible error she had
made in falling in love with him.

Over the following days, Evan took her to historic
places, to the Black Forest with its wooded hills,
streams and villages. They strolled through medieval
towns and drove to the river Rhine, where they walked
along its banks, visiting its picturesque towns along
the way.

They clambered high over the Lorelei, the rock
which overlooked the river and which, according to
legend, was the home of a siren whose song lured
boatmen to their doom. They climbed steep hills to
visit castles and gazed down upon the busy river
traffic.

They visited the forests and the sandstone hills of
the Odenwald, lunching first and satisfyingly in a
restaurant with a tiled floor and stout wooden chairs
and pot plants everywhere.

Parking the car again, they climbed a path through
sun-dappled woods where they found the *Felsenmeer*,
the Sea of Rocks which tumbled incredibly downward

between tall-reaching pine trees. The great stones and boulders, Evan explained, had come from glacial action millions of years ago, and there they remained. The Romans had used the stones, carving them, indenting them with teeth-like patterns. There was even a column of stone lying there and it was as if the Romans had been interrupted in their work and had been called away—for ever.

At Rothenburg ob der Tauber, an ancient medieval town on the river Tauber, they wandered hand-in-hand through the cobbled streets. Fran marvelled at the half-timbered houses with their decorative gables, window boxes spilling over with flowers and the secret, arched passageways leading off in all directions.

At a Konditorei, they feasted on *Kaffee und Kuchen* beneath a waterfall of ivy-green fronds cascading down from balustraded galleries. They had chosen the gateaux, rich with cream, from a dish at the counter. Fran put down her fork and delicately licked each finger, unwilling to leave a single piece untasted.

At the end of the fourth day's sightseeing, she collapsed on to the long settee near the window and felt the excitement of the past hours still throbbing in her veins.

Evan dropped beside her and pulled her into his arms. Their mouths knew the way to each other no matter how intense the darkness might be. Each night they had made love, slept, then loved again. To Fran, they had been days of unimaginable happiness, made even more intense by the knowledge that, inevitably, they would have to end.

The 'pretence' of loving had become so much of a reality that she did not know how she would ever be able to change back to pretending to be indifferent and emotionally cold.

Lifting his head, Evan asked, 'Have you seen

enough now to decide which backgrounds you'll use for your fashion pictures?'

Fran nodded, her eyes dreamy as they traced the strong line of his jaw. Her finger moved up to make contact and he smiled lazily, turning his mouth. As his teeth nipped her finger-tips, she squealed, snatching her hand away. He put her off his lap, moving to sit cornerwise and propping an elbow on the settee back. Fran held still. Almost imperceptibly, the atmosphere was changing. A moment later, she knew the cause and her heart sank.

'I have Willa's address,' Evan said quietly. 'She's free at a moment's notice to come over to model the clothes.'

It wasn't happening, it couldn't be, not so soon, snatching her happiness from her.

Taking a breath and with an effort controlling her voice, she said,

'I take it you're talking as my boss now?'

'You've taken it right.'

'But——' she faltered under the power of his eyes, 'but even as my employer——' how ridiculous that sounded now they were lovers, 'you have no right to dictate to me which models I do or don't use.'

He looked at her steadily.

Probably, Fran thought, just leaving me to flounder. Which she proceeded to do, since she simply did not know how to deal with the situation. 'I've already told you that Willa Hemming's style isn't in line with that of the magazine.'

'Your style will become her style,' he replied levelly. 'Where her work is concerned, she's entirely professional.'

Fran stood up, unable to remain seated in the face of his goading words. 'You still love her,' she accused. 'You must do, you speak so well of her. So why did you marry me?'

He rose, too, towering over her. It was as though the past few wonderful days had never been. 'Love, in the sense you use it, has no existence in my world. Which, as you know, is why I married you.'

'But——' A swallow of breath stopped the truth from pouring out. She was face to face with the consequences of her stupidity. She was now as vulnerable as anyone else who fell in love. It was like a great rock poised above her head. If Evan chose to roll it down—indulge in those extra-marital affairs he said would be part of their marriage—then she would go over and over to rock-bottom, as wounded and crushed as any other person whose love had been thrown in their face. Like her mother and her father . . .

She swayed and closed her eyes. 'Please excuse me.' He did not try to stop her.

In the bedroom, she put fingers to her temples, forcing herself to calm down. He had said to her—she remembered now; how could she ever have forgotten it?—'Provided the pretence ends as soon as the so-called honeymoon is over'.

There was a sound and she turned, startled. He had been watching her from the doorway—for how long?

'I anticipated your opposition,' he said, tone incisive—the blade of the 'penknife' side of his personality was in good cutting form, 'and made the appropriate arrangements on your behalf. My *ex-wife*,' he made the word into a taunt, 'is arriving tomorrow.'

CHAPTER SEVEN

FRAN awoke to an imprint on the pillow beside hers. For the first time in days, the night had passed without a touch or a word, except 'good night'.

Around four o'clock, Evan had left the bed and had not returned. Fran had lain there listening and waiting, then had opened the door to find him seated in the living-room surrounded by papers. He had preferred to work, rather than lie beside her.

She lay on her back watching the shadows turn into shapes. Her whole body had longed for his touch, she had become attuned to him in every possible way. Again, she felt the terrible consequences of her foolishness in falling for him, in losing control of her emotions—the very thing she had sworn would never happen to her and the reason, or so she had told herself, why she had agreed to marry him.

Looking back, she knew the process had begun at their first meeting. The initial attraction, the curious sensations she had experienced while with him, the hastened heart beats—all these were explained now in one simple statement. She had fallen in love.

It had started that far back, yet she had blinded herself to the fact, told herself it was physical attraction. She rolled on to her front and propped up her forehead with her palms. Her assumptions had all been so wrong, so disastrously wrong!

'Fran.'

He rarely shortened her name and she stiffened without turning. Her answering 'Yes?' was muffled by the pillow.

'I'm going to my office in Frankfurt.' He paused, plainly expecting an answer. He went on, 'It's about half an hour's drive. I keep a car for use when I'm here.'

'So the honeymoon's over.' Fran listened to the words she had not meant to speak and pressed her lips together.

He must have come silently over the soft carpet. He turned her ungently and she flopped on to her back. 'The honeymoon is over.' He repeated the words with clarity. She had been put in her place—a nuisance, a mere diversion, both a stimulator and an appeaser of his sexual appetite. His eyes weaved a way along her body. Her night attire was filmy and brief. For the past nights she had worn nothing, but last night she had felt the need of some kind of barrier, flimsy though it was.

He sat beside her, sliding a careless arm beneath her shoulders, lightly holding her breast. 'Sulky, petulant, stormy-eyed—it makes no difference. You're still too bloody attractive for a man's peace of mind.'

'A man's', he'd said, she noted, not 'my peace of mind'. She shut her eyes on him, felt the pressure and the tongue-movement of an almost contemptuous, invasive kiss, then it was over. Her body protested at the sudden withdrawal of intimate contact.

He spoke again at the door, 'If you want to contact your deputy in London, feel free to use the telephone.' He was gone before she could ask him when he would be back.

Fran took the tram into the town, travelling along the wide streets with their tree-lined pavements watched over by balconies with bright sunshades and adorned with flowers. The shutters had been pushed wide open to the sun.

It was more than a wish to sightsee that had

encouraged her to leave the apartment; it was also the knowledge that soon she would be forced to play hostess to Willa Hemming. She had contacted Judy, her deputy, telling her to send a photographer and the clothes she required for the modelling sessions. She would, she said, supplement them with styles she would by then have found where she was staying.

Finding herself in the town centre, she wandered in the spring sunshine around the shops and large stores surrounding Luisenplatz with its high column of stone on which perched a statue of Ernst Ludwig. Using a German phrase book, Fran made some purchases, then took a seat at an open air café in the Rheinstrasse.

The spacious paved area reflected back the sun's warmth and Fran watched the people seated in the white-painted chairs and tables. They were drinking coffee, soaking up the sun, chatting or reading newspapers, some people having ordered the delicious pastries of which Fran had seen so many varieties since her arrival.

The sight of them took her back to the café in Rothenburg, where she and Evan had shared coffee and cakes. He had shown her the all-year Christmas Shop, with its giant ground-to-upper-floor fir tree covered in lights, while the shop's shelves overflowed with Christmas gifts available uninterruptedly from one year's end to the next.

He had bought her whatever she had pointed to or exclaimed over and she had talked of putting them away in their festive wrappings until the following December when he could give them to her all over again. The stars had been in her eyes that day, she thought, stirring the coffee she had ordered. She had had the foolishness to assume that they would spend Christmastime that year together.

Then, she had only to lift her eyes and he had been

there, across the table. Now there was an empty seat. Which, she reflected, was how it was likely to be for as long as their married life lasted. The honeymoon was over, he had said. And there was only one honeymoon per marriage, wasn't there?

'*Frau* Dowd?' The tall, fair-haired man smiled down at her. 'You are looking sad. May I perhaps cheer you up?'

Fran laughed and expressed to Dietmar her pleasure at seeing him, which was genuine. For such a beautiful day, her thoughts had been too sombre even for her own good.

He pulled out a chair, ordering coffee from the waiter who had come at his request, adding another cup for Fran.

'I have just come from your husband's Frankfurt office. My father and I—we have been talking business again with Evan.'

Fran nodded, asking, 'Are things going well?'

'For whom,' he asked comically, 'for the sellers or the buyers?' He waved her apology away. 'My father and I are in agreement about selling. But for my grandfather—it goes—you say something like—against the grain?'

'And Sabina? I mean, *Fraulein* Richter?'

He made a face. 'Our so beautiful financial adviser. She is,' he rocked his open hand from side to side, 'half and half, for and against. She wants a good price. Sometimes, I think it is more than your Dowd board are prepared to pay. But she and your husband, they get on,' he paused, seeming to consider his words and giving her a covert glance. 'Er——' he cleared his throat, 'quite well.' It was, to Fran's ears, a carefully tactful statement.

Fran drained her coffee cup, watching its slow descent to the saucer. So her suspicions about them had not been without foundation. Those 'long dark hours' to which Sabina had referred, she thought with painful sarcasm, had clearly been used to further their closer acquaintance.

'You know *Fraulein* Richter well?' she asked.

A wide shoulder lifted nonchalantly. 'A long time ago,' was the noncommital reply. 'We were too young. It is over . . .'

Is it? Fran wondered. 'Do you live here?' she asked, breaking the brief silence.

'*Nein*. I have friends in Darmstadt. Unfortunately, they were out. Or maybe fortunately,' his smile was happy, 'since I have met you. Have you seen the sights it has to offer? You have not? What has your husband Evan been doing for the past few days?'

'Showing me the favourite tourists' haunts in this part of Germany. There are some beautiful places.'

Dietmar nodded. 'And here in this city, there are woods and forests within walking distance. There is the Orangery built in 1719.' He was counting on his fingers. 'There is the Prince George's Palace and the beautiful, gilded Russian chapel built for Tsar Nicholas the Second, not forgetting the Mathildenhöhe, with its so-called Wedding Tower which resembles the five fingers of a hand.'

Fran smiled. 'So much all at once. I'm interested for other reasons, too. I'm looking for background for some fashion modelling, and——'

'I will take you.' Dietmar jumped up impulsively. 'Right now. Come, *Frau*——' He paused, head on one side. 'May I call you——?'

She nodded. 'Fran, please. And I'm not quite ready for more sightseeing. You see, I must have the model, the clothes——'

'But what are these?' He indicated the large carrier bags on the ground around the table.

'These are some, but there'll be more, sent across from London, hopefully in the care of the photographer.' She glanced at her watch. 'I really must be going. Any time now I'm expecting Evan's——' What was she thinking of? Evan obviously wanted his first marriage kept a secret, and she had nearly let it out! 'The lady—the model—she's arriving today, but I don't know what time.' Fran was collecting her baggage. 'I must go back. To Evan's apartment, I mean. It was so nice meeting you, *Herr* Müller——'

'My name is Dietmar, please. Where did you park your car?'

She shook her head, murmuring, 'Tram.'

'Oh, but I will take you back. I will not hear of your travelling by public transport when I have a car and my time at your service.' He was hurrying her towards the entrance of a multi-storeyed car park, having relieved her of most of her bags and carriers.

He knew where Evan's apartment was. He had, he said, visited it not so long ago. He looked around as they walked from the parking area and made for the apartment block. 'She is not wandering around, that lady model. Perhaps she is playing on the children's swings?' His grin made Fran laugh.

She also experienced a sense of profound relief that the woman had not yet arrived. Maybe she wouldn't come after all. Maybe Evan had only said it to annoy her . . .

Even before she turned the key, Fran heard the telephone ringing. Dropping everything to the floor, she hurried to silence the sound. 'Fran here. I'm sorry, I mean—*Ich bin Frau Dowd* . . .'

'*Ja?*' There followed a jumble of words which had Fran groping for comprehension. She looked at the 'phone, turned to Dietmar and held it out. 'It's in German. Please?'

Dietmar smiled and spoke. '*Vielleicht kann Ich Ihnen helfen?*' He frowned, then burst out laughing. 'This is Dietmar. I will give you back your wife.' He said, returning the receiver, 'It is your husband, playing a trick on you.'

'Why did you do that?' Fran rebuked Evan. 'You know I can't speak a word——'

'What's Müller doing there?'

The laughter he had shared with Dietmar had gone. 'He bought me coffee, brought me back here.'

'Did you arrange to meet him?'

'If I did, what of it?' she prevaricated against her better judgment. His unpleasantness and suspicion so soon after the sweetness of their lovemaking angered her. She would anger him back. 'There's nothing to stop me, under the conditions of our marr——' Dietmar was there, she could not quarrel with Evan within his hearing, nor let him know the unusual circumstances of their marriage.

The silence was like a garden rake running over her ear. At last, he said, his voice voice grating, 'Haven't you heard the one about not committing misdemeanours outside your own front door?'

'This isn't *my* front door and in any case, I haven't done anything——' Wrong, she had been going to say, but, she thought, why should I set his mind at rest? Didn't he say that our marriage would be an 'open' one? 'Yet,' she added with conscious provocation.

'I've had a call from Willa.' He spoke as if his teeth were clenched. 'She's arriving by a later plane than expected. I'm meeting her.' The 'phone was rammed down, making Fran's ear tremble.

For a few moments she did not turn, trying to compose herself. Then she produced a bright smile. 'Will you take a seat? Would you like a drink?'

Dietmar shook his head. 'You need not bother to entertain me. I think maybe you are upset?'

'No, I——' Fran saw the parcels and bent to gather them. Returning from the bedroom where she had tidied the clothes away, she asked, 'Shall I cook some lunch? Would you like to stay?'

He was shaking his head even as she spoke. 'You will allow me to buy you a meal, then take you to those places we talked about? You would like that?'

'Very much. Then I could decide which of them to use as background for the fashion pictures.' It would also stop her from brooding all the rest of the day about Willa Hemming's imminent arrival.

Dietmar took her to a *gaststätte* where, he explained, a meal could be ordered together with drinks. There were long wooden tables set with place mats, while other tables were hidden away in alcoves. The plates were piled with food and when the waiter put the plate in front of her, Fran discovered she was hungry.

'*Guten Appetit*,' the waiter said and Fran nodded her appreciation.

Afterwards, Dietmar took her sightseeing, driving through woods at the summit of which the Schloss Auerbach stood proudly, its turrets and towers glowing against the blue sky.

Sunlight sparkled through branches on to last year's bracken and there was a glimpse of a view stretching beyond steep bends and runaway slopes, while the trees' trunks grew so close together, Fran commented they resembled beaded curtains.

At the Burg Frankenstein, they walked along stone-flagged paths and gazed over the castle's walls towards the Rhine and into the far distance. Then they had coffee and cakes beneath striped umbrellas shading them from the sun's bright rays.

Some people, Dietmar said, considered that the

castle Frankenstein may well have been the ancestral
seat of a noble family, even, maybe, having links with
the famous horror-film monster.

As they drove back to the apartment, Fran's mind
turned back the hours to her edgy conversation with
Evan. Then her thoughts sped forward and she
foresaw with dread the evening of waiting and
wondering that lay ahead. When Dietmar drove into
the multi-storey car park and asked, 'Will you let me
take you for a meal?' she started to shake her head,
then thought, Why should I play the tame, neglected
wife?

'I have a better idea,' she answered, her smile
determinedly bright. 'I offered you lunch but you said
no, so——?' She gestured towards the apartment block
which they were approaching, the key in her hand.

'Now how can I refuse a second time?' Dietmar
remarked, smiling. 'But your husband will not like an
unexpected guest.'

The possibility had darted in—and out—of her
mind but she had told herself defiantly that she didn't
really care, so she shook her head, dismissing the idea.

There was food in the fridge and some chilled wine.
While she cooked, Dietmar set two places at the table.
Afterwards, they drank coffee in the evening sun on
the balcony overlooking the view. In one of the few
silences—they had talked almost non-stop about the
world of magazine publishing—her mind played a
trick and substituted Evan for Dietmar.

Then the thought came that if Evan had indeed
been there they would not have been sitting talking.
They would have been making love . . . The memory
of his kisses, of his arms about her holding her
intimately not so many hours before brought a wave of
nostalgia so strong she had deliberately to tense her
muscles and fight it off. With jerking movements, she

rose and collected the empty cups, at which Dietmar immediately helped, carrying the tray into the kitchen.

It was almost dark now and the speed of her heartbeats had increased as the minutes had passed, not in excitement so much as a kind of gripping fear. Where was Evan, she wondered. Was he waiting about at the airport or had Willa arrived and he had taken her—where?

'I can see you're tired,' Dietmar was saying. 'I will go. You will be okay? Evan will come home soon? Or would you like me to stay until he does?'

'Thanks, but no.' She smiled her gratitude for his understanding. 'Thank you for today.'

He smiled back, taking her hand. 'It was just a preliminary. When will you want me to take you around for the photography?'

'Maybe tomorrow?' He nodded. 'The fashion model will have arrived by then. If the weather's good—shall we say ten o'clock?'

'It shall be exactly then. Good night, now, and,' he squeezed her hand and released it at last, 'do not be so worried. Your husband will soon return.'

Fran closed the door and leaned against it, wishing she could be as sure as Dietmar that Evan would come back soon.

A sudden tiredness hit her. The long day without Evan, the weariness of the seemingly interminable wait to see him again had taken its toll. She longed to put things right between them and tell him she had not meant a word of what she had implied on the telephone.

The evening was still relatively early and she decided to clear away the dishes later, taking a shower first to help her relax. She was pulling on her lavender velvet wrap when she heard a door open and a woman laughing.

'Evan,' the visitor said, 'it's so wonderful to be with you again——' There was a quick silence. 'What's wrong, darling?' came on a note of surprise. 'Oh, I see you're objecting to the mess. You seem to have got yourself an untidy wife second time round.'

The door of the bedroom was swung open and closed, and Evan's eyes swept round the room.

'Where's Müller?' he rasped.

A twisting fury shot through Fran's body at the implied insult. 'He heard you coming and slipped out the back way,' she hurled at him, only to cry out as his hand caught her arms in a brutal grip.

Her white face stared up at him, recoiling at the cruelty in the hard line of his mouth. He began to speak, changed his mind and threw her from him as if he could not bear to touch her. Then he turned and went from the room.

All those hours, Fran thought, holding herself where his fingers had bruised her, waiting for him to come home so that she could tell him she hadn't meant what she'd said earlier that day. Then, when he did return, she made things worse by hitting back at him in exactly the same way. But, she thought, swallowing her tears, he had insulted her and no woman with any pride could have let that pass.

There was a clatter of crockery. Willa called, singingly, 'It's okay, darling, I'll clear these things. I'll be a better wife to you as your woman than I ever was as your legal spouse!'

Fran clapped her hands over her ears. Let them get on with it, she thought, with a defiance that, as the minutes went by, grew increasingly thin.

'Willa,' it was Evan calling now, 'how do you like your steak? I've forgotten.'

'Evan, sweetie, I'll never forgive you for your terrible memory loss. Rare, darling, rare. Now do you remember?'

A radio was switched on, the delicious aroma of food crept under the door. The raised voices, the throbbing sound of music, the intermittent bursts of laughter drove Fran to roll the bed cover around her head and clench her fists on the pillow.

She was taken back over the weeks to the party in the chalet. When his guests had gone, Evan had come in to see her, helped her into bed, made her skin come to life at his touch. He had demanded again an answer to his marriage proposal. She had been determined to give him her answer, had tried to say 'no', but the refusal just hadn't come.

Even then, she realised she had known. Despite all her protestations to him that she would never become emotionally involved with a man, she had, without realising it, been in love with him.

The knowledge gave her no comfort now. At the chalet she had fallen asleep waiting, but for what she had not then known. Now she knew the reason, but this time he did not appear. All the time the party for two went on, she waited. When the silence she had been dreading finally came, she waited. In the end, she fell asleep with her head on his pillow and dreamed that he was in her arms.

CHAPTER EIGHT

It was six o'clock when she awoke. Her sleep had
been light and she knew that all night the silence
had not been broken. There was a pain inside her
that even the clean brightness of the morning did
not wash away.

Fran dressed quickly and went into the lobby,
looking at the bedroom doors. If one had been open,
she would have known at once where Evan had spent
the night but both were closed and this told her
nothing. A soft moan reached her ears, a murmured,
'Darling,' a rustle of bedclothes, then the silence
returned.

It was enough. Fran snatched a jacket from the coat
stand and wrenched open the entrance door. The lift
would have been quicker, but the stairs beckoned.
Using them would work off the anger and the pain.

The main road was busy even at that hour, the
trams hummed along the side of the broad street.
Crossing, Fran broke away into some woods. An early
cyclist whistled his cheerful way past, a bird swooped
low, an aircraft droned overhead. There was a circular
shelter and Fran made for it, sitting on the curving
bench and looking abstractedly at her skirt as the new
day's sun threw its own dappled shadows across it.

She had to face the inevitable. For her, it was the
end of their marriage. In the truest sense, she told
herself. When a legal bond had been proposed, she
had accepted on the grounds of 'no ties'. Now Evan
had begun to indulge in the right they had agreed
upon—an extra-marital affair—she knew that, as a

result of her own personal discovery, she couldn't take it.

Now that she knew she loved him, the whole arrangement had become unworkable. The irony made her wince, then want to cry. Why, why did it have to be with his ex-wife, the woman who, by her desertion of him just after the wedding ceremony, had made him look upon all women as worthless?

Letting herself into the apartment, she paused to listen. It seemed that the silence still held. Had their satisfaction with each other been so intense? Removing her jacket, Fran went into the kitchen—and stopped in her tracks. Seated at the table was Evan, papers spread before him. So he was not still lying in Willa's arms, as she had supposed.

He did not look up as Fran entered. Although the morning was warm, she could not suppress a shiver. The coffee was percolating and she could not tell whether he had provided for two cups or three. That silence had to be broken.

'Evan?' His name came from a dry throat. He moved but did not answer. 'Is there enough here for me?'

His head came round slowly, his eyes cold under raised brows. 'There's more than enough for you—room in my residences, cash in my banks.'

Fran felt her cheeks drain. 'Are you giving me notice to quit your life?'

He threw down his pen. 'I would have thought that that was what you wanted. However, that is not what I'm saying. I'm merely telling you that the conditions under which we agreed to marry still hold good. You can have your affairs, I have mine.'

'And you're having one right now, under this roof.'

'Aren't you?'

'No, no I'm not! What I implied last night wasn't true.'

He clasped his hands, one elbow resting on the back
of the wooden bench seat. 'So now you know we're
quits—an affair each, as it were—you're trying to deny
yours so as to put me in the wrong?'

Fran's agitation increased. 'I'm not trying to deny
it, I am denying it. There's nothing between myself
and Dietmar, you have to believe me.'

His broad shoulders lifted and settled. 'Whether I
do or I don't is largely irrelevant. We were under no
illusions when we married each other. There was no
love between us, which is a situation that persists, as
far as I'm concerned.' He went back to his work,
starting to write. 'I'm just surprised at Müller, that's
all.'

'I tell you, there's nothing.' Fran gripped his
shoulder, shook it. The muscles contracted and with a
swift, decisive movement, he closed over her hand and
threw it from him. Again he was treating her as
though he had soiled his skin by touching her. Fran
nursed her hand and put it to her cheek.

'All he talked about,' she said, 'when it wasn't
business, was Sabina. They loved each other once, did
you know?' Evan went on writing. 'But you wouldn't
bother yourself with such trivialities, would you?
Sabina's one of your women, too, isn't she. I've
noticed the likeness between her and your wife——'
She drew back at the look in his eyes. 'Your—your ex-
wife . . .'

He had half-risen from the seat, his body
menacingly angled. 'Get out. Get back to your
man——'

'Darling!' The very feminine wail came from behind
a closed bedroom door. 'You've been away from me
too long. Stop quarrelling with your current wife and
come back to your past one. I told you, darling,' the
door opened and Willa posed provocatively in a scarlet

satin robe, 'I'm getting divorced from Ken and we can get together again. Ah, Mrs Dowd,' her eyes slewed to Fran, 'Evan can be so *maddening* when he likes, can't he? So icy he freezes you up, but when he gets going, you melt and he just *drinks* you. There, darling, do you like my poetry?' She floated across to Evan's side and rested her clasped hands on his shoulder, leaning her graceful body against him.

He did not push her away. He tolerated her but the anger did not leave his face. Fran turned from the tableau, wanting to tear the other woman's hair but showing nothing of her anguish. She went into the bedroom and closed the door. She made two brief 'phone calls, one apologetic, the other with authority. Then she pulled her cases from hiding and began filling them.

'Going somewhere?' Evan was in the doorway.

'Obeying your orders,' Fran threw back, 'getting out.'

He moved in a few paces. 'You look pale. If you can't take it, you shouldn't have accepted my proposal of a loveless marriage.'

She did not answer, just went on mechanically packing.

'You used the 'phone.'

'I did.' Her white face held defiance. 'I told Dietmar not to come this morning. He was going to take your w——' She had so nearly said it again! 'Take the *model* and myself around today for the fashion pictures. I can see you don't believe me, any more than you did earlier. Ask him yourself.'

'I believe you. I believe he would do anything for you. I watched the two of you at the working dinner.'

'And I watched you and Sabina.' He did not respond to her taunt. 'The other call was to London, cancelling the photographer who was arriving at

Frankfurt airport this morning.' She looked around dully for anything she might have overlooked. 'I'll have to leave you to tell Miss Hemming about the cancelled modelling sessions. If she's short of money, she can claim for wasted expenses. I expect the company will be lenient where an *ex*-relative of one of its top men is concerned.'

His hands were on her arms again and she winced as his fingers fitted over the bruises he had inflicted a few hours earlier.

Through his teeth, he said, 'Leave the sarcasm to me.'

She twisted free, crying, 'It wasn't sarcasm, I was simply being practical.' Which she told herself, was partially true. Smoothing her hair, she bent to pick up her cases.

'How do I look?'

Fran glanced up, her hands empty. Willa, on cue as usual, had advanced into the bedroom wearing one of the outfits Fran had bought the previous day. Her blonde hair had been swept to one side and her hands were on her slender hips which she had swung provocatively. She changed her pose, moved her eyes sideways and asked, 'Well?'

Mentally, automatically, Fran drew a page around her. So Evan had been right. Your style will become Willa's style, he'd said, she's entirely professional. He should know, Fran thought acidly, she was his woman for long enough.

Well, she was not going to let Willa off so easily. 'Your image is glossy and classical,' she pointed out. 'I told Evan I was not convinced you could adapt to the style of *Woman's Choice*.'

'When I model, I also act,' Willa snapped. 'I take on the personality of the clothes I'm wearing.'

Fran allowed herself to nod. 'I see that Evan's faith

in you was justified. I——' she glanced at him, 'I'll bear you in mind the next time the fashion feature of the magazine needs a model.'

'What do you mean? That's what I'm here for, isn't it?'

Fran glanced at Evan, then back at Willa but it seemed he had no intention of taking his cue.

'I'm sorry,' Fran said, 'but I've changed my mind about the photo session.'

'I need the job, the money that goes with it.' Willa was not acting now.

'I'm sorry.' This time the suitcases were safely in Fran's grasp. 'I expect Evan will help you out financially. After all, he's the boss of the company.'

Fran discovered that her lower lip showed a marked tendency to tremble and she became aware that her control was slipping. Much more, she thought, horrified, and I'll be weeping on Evan's shoulder, one that was hard and unyielding, but wonderful to rest a cheek against . . .

'I walked out on him too,' Willa was saying. 'All right, so I'd just got his ring on my finger, but I realised too late I couldn't take his ice-cold core any longer.'

Fran thought, keeping her face averted, once he talked about *my* ice and *his* fire. Now the situation had been reversed. It hurts, she told herself, with a terrible intensity . . .

'Know Müller's address?' The question came drily from Evan.

Fran shot him a frowning look.

'Why should I know it?'

Willa shook her head in sympathy and withdrew into the bedroom.

'Who else would you be running to?' Evan persisted.

'I'm not running *to* anyone.'

'So you're running *from* me?' Those tantalisingly dependable shoulders lifted and fell. 'Don't bother. We can go our own ways under the same roof.'

The statement, with its terrible ring of finality made her go cold. A broken marriage . . . Now I know, she thought, momentarily closing her eyes, how my mother felt, and my father. And it hurts, it hurts unbearably.

Without a glance back, she made for the lift. The traffic in the busy road sped by with daunting anonymity. She thought she saw a taxi. Forgetting she was in another country, she lifted her hand and stepped off the kerb. A squeal of brakes made her head swing and she realised that the traffic drove on an unfamiliar side of the road.

At the last minute, she took a step back. It was too late—contact was made, a bruising, breath-robbing impact and she felt her body hit the ground. There were voices, lights glaring in her terrified eyes, then nothing.

'Where were you going?' The question came at her out of the mist. The speaker seemed so far away. She just had to be somewhere else. The ground was never as soft as this.

It was Evan's bed, in Evan's apartment. It came back now, everything that had happened to her. 'To Frankfurt. The airport. Didn't have a flight booked. Knew I'd have to wait.'

The phrases came out jerkily. Someone else seemed to be speaking but with her voice. Her mind was all right, she decided with relief. It was her aching, tender body that was giving trouble.

Her eyes focused on the coolly handsome face above her. How could she make that aloof man smile? 'I'm sorry,' she gestured towards herself, 'about all this.

I'm not normally accident prone——'

'You said that once before. Just after you'd collected a bang on the head from a set of skis.'

'You remember?'

'How could I forget? It was the first of two calamities at the chalet.'

'There were three.' Evan looked puzzled. 'The other was meeting——' She cut off the words. Meeting Willa again, she had been going to say. But if it hadn't happened there, it would have happened some time. Willa would have sought him out wherever he was. She intended remarrying him, didn't she?

Fran looked painfully around. 'Where's your—I mean, Miss Hemming?'

'Nearly said it, didn't you?' he asked drily. 'Staying at a nearby hotel.'

'You needn't have pushed her out of here for me. Or,' she eyed him dully, aware of the aches and pains again, 'is it more convenient to have her there? I mean, you wouldn't be committing adultery at your own front door, then, would you?'

Her flickering eyelids shut out the thinning of his lips. When his hand rested, none too gently, on her bare shoulder, she looked at him, startled.

'Getting mown down by a passing car hasn't knocked the sarcasm out of you.' His pressure on her flesh lifted a little and the hold turned into a near-caress. She felt her arm coming to life, then shuddering under the ache of the bruising.

'It hurts.' Her brow pleated in a worried frown. 'What happened to me?'

'Grazing and light injuries. Fortunately no more than that. Apparently, your self-preserving instinct took you back a few paces, which was sufficient to protect you from serious trouble.'

She nodded, thinking, I wish that instinct had come into play when I first met you. My life wouldn't be in the mess it is now.

'The doctor came,' Evan went on. 'After a few moments of unconsciousness, you came round briefly, then went to sleep on us. He said you must rest in bed.'

She tried a smile. 'I've heard that before, too. The doctor at the chalet . . .'

His smile joined hers, but his did not last. 'The doctor suggested a warm bath to ease the discomfort. Only if you feel like it, of course.'

'I'd love one.' She pushed aside the cover, pulled it up again. Someone had removed most of her clothes. 'You?' she asked, feeling oddly shy in front of the man who was her husband. The hours since they had shared the same bed seemed to have stretched into days and weeks, turning him into almost a stranger.

'Who else?' he answered languidly. 'At least agree that I have a legal right to see you naked.'

He was referring, Fran realised, to her supposed 'lover', Dietmar Müller.

'I don't know what you're talking about,' she returned angrily.

A wave of weariness came at her through the nagging pain of her injuries, light though they were considered to be. 'I'll give the bath a miss,' she told him, turning her face aside.

He left her and a few moments later, there was a rushing of water. He was filling the bath for her!

'Right.' He appeared at the adjoining door, rolling up his sleeves.

'No, thank you, I've decided I don't——' Her lips parted releasing a gasp.

He was uncovering her, tugging at the remaining clothes and lifting her, despite her protests. His gaze

stroked her tingling body and his mouth lowered to
kiss the injured places. His eyes were passion-filled
but there was no warmth in his expression.

Her forehead found his chest and she hid from him
the dismay she felt at his intransigence. 'I told you,'
she declared, her voice muffled, 'there's only friend-
liness between Dietmar and me. But even if there was
more than that,' she lifted her head, remembering last
night when he had gone to Willa instead of herself,
'our marriage is an open one, isn't it? If you can enjoy
extra-marital affairs, then so can——'

His mouth was a hard line. 'If you have any sense,'
he said, his fingers gripping her flesh, 'you'll stop
provoking me until you're no longer at my mercy.'

He suspended her over the bath and she tensed,
holding her breath for his revenge, for the impact of
either chilled or over-heated water. Instead, he
lowered her into the soothing, temperate bathwater
with a tenderness that almost made her cry. She
squeezed the sponge but he took it away and soaped
his hands.

'I can manage,' she whispered, fearful of her body's
reaction if he touched her.

He knelt on one knee, smoothing his soaped palms
across her shoulders, moving down over the spreading
bruises on her arms and hips. Upwards again to her
throat, holding her chin high and forcing her to look
into the desire his eyes contained.

Slowly, his hands slipped down, moulding her
breasts and massaging the thrusting nipple with his
thumbs.

Her damp lips forced themselves into a pouting plea
and with a sudden movement, he bent to hold them
with his. When he released them, they stayed apart
and moist, almost as if they were asking for more, but
their request was not granted.

He renewed the soap and moved to her legs, lifting each one and lathering them with care and gentleness, studying the sore places one by one. He found her thighs, moving minutely upwards, tearing from her the words,

'No, Evan, please. I'll wash myself.'

His smile was enigmatic, and he took no notice at all. His hands went higher, to places that had her teeth making indentations on her lower lip and small, pleading sounds coming from her throat. Her pulses were throbbing, his arousal almost driving her mad.

She seized his hand and dragged it to her mouth, kissing his fingers and his palm until her face was moist with the water which clung to them. For a few moments, he tolerated her kisses, then he firmly disengaged his hand, an action which brought a frown of frustration to Fran's flushed cheeks.

He took the giant bath towel from the heated rail, lifting her out and wrapping it round her. He ran his fingers through her curling hair, sweeping it back so that it hung down.

'Let me dry myself,' she urged and there was a plea in the cry.

He ignored it as he had ignored all her other plaintive requests. His palms swept down over her slenderness, then up again, but gently all the while, remembering the tender places.

'Where's your nightgown?' The words were spoken with unnerving harshness and she realised that his gentleness stemmed only from consideration, not from any deeper feeling. He found it, slipping it over her head.

In the early hours, she woke to find tears on her cheeks. He came quickly from the room he had been occupying. It was plain he had not been sleeping. He was dressed in shirt and trousers and there was a mask of fatigue across his features.

He gazed down at her. 'Well?' he asked. Couldn't he, she thought with despair, unbend towards me even at this time of night? 'You must have called me for something.'

'I'm sorry,' she scrubbed at the tears with the sheet. 'I didn't know I had. I was dreaming.' She rubbed at her hair. 'Of you.' She hadn't meant to tell him. 'The dream was better than the real man. Go away.' Tugging the cover over her shoulders and her profile, she clamped her eyelids down, lashes sweeping over the shadows underlining her eyes.

The next thing she knew was the feel of his hands moving her round. Something was being removed, over her head, then came the feel of him again, naked to her nakedness, and she was in his arms, her skin trembling against his.

'No, no, I—we—you'll hurt my bruises . . .' Why am I protesting, she wondered. It's what I want, what I was dreaming about.

'I'll be considerate and gentle.' His lips moved against her throat, his hands held her breasts, imprisoning them so that his mouth could make free with them one after the other. Her hands ran feverishly over his neck, his shoulders, his wide, strong back. Her thighs opened to his, her body was asking him, inviting him, please take me, love me.

He felt its urgent message, moved on to her and into her and her thoughts soared like skylarks, singing madly, glad that once again he had turned to her and wanted her and only her . . . There was a burst of joy, an explosion of loving, slowly ebbing to a depth of tranquillity she had never known before.

Sleep came, deep and refreshing and her dreams that had become reality in turn became dreams again, but this time there was love between them and warmth and shared laughter which bound as surely as shared passion.

When she awoke, daylight had come. Her hand reached out and rested on a mound of hip bone. In the night he hadn't left her, he had stayed at her side. His arm came out even as he slept and wound around her breasts, pulling her backwards and against him. 'You're my woman and you'll stay, you won't get away.'

He was talking to her in his sleep, telling her of his need of her—of her what? Her womanhood, the satisfaction she gave to his male desire? His woman, he'd called her, but she was his wife! So had it been Willa he'd talked to in his dream?

It was vital now to sort the facts from the fantasies, the truth from the dreams. She had to remember, must never forget, that he took his pleasure from other women, too. And because their marriage was based on freedom to take other lovers, this was something she had to accept.

What, she despaired, had happened to that vow of hers to stay forever uninvolved? To take part only in impassioned, but coldly deliberate, sexual interludes? Why hadn't she realised that in practice it would for her be an impossibility?

She pushed away from Evan's arms and surprisingly he let her go. In making such a vow, she told herself she had shown an unforgivable lack of self-knowledge. Hadn't she realised that her nature was warm and capable of deep affection? Why had she needed to come this far to recognise her own, true character? That nothing less than an intensely loving relationship would suffice? Bitter tears salted her cheeks and lips and again the sheet dried them, but did not stop their flow.

Compelling fingers turned her face, making her look upwards into Evan's dark gaze. 'Crying because you found me beside you and not the man you really wanted?' He jerked his hand away and went from the bed.

The irony made her maul her lower lip and rub the back of her hand across her eyes. She was crying because he'd made love to her without affection and because the love she felt for him could never be shown. And because there wasn't any other man on earth she could love as she loved Evan Dowd. Yet he believed she wanted to change him for another man!

It was no time at all before he had showered and dressed. He came to look down at her, suitcase in his hand.

Which, Fran reasoned, could only mean one thing. He was leaving her. 'Where——' She moistened her lips. 'Where are you going?'

'New York. A business trip. Fortuitously, as it happens, since I'm leaving the field clear, which is plainly what you want.'

She saw the angry brilliance of his eyes and her heart sank. 'Clear for whom?'

'Whichever man you were breaking your heart over earlier. Your tears told me I had the wrong face, the wrong body, the wrong name. Now, the lover you prefer, whoever he is, can come and go as often as you wish.' He ignored the shake of her head and glanced at his watch. 'I have a plane to catch. From Frankfurt.'

She felt moisture forming on her palms. It was true, he *was* leaving her. 'Where will you be? I mean, if I should want to get in touch?'

'Why should you? Go ahead, live with the man. Our marriage holds, no matter how many lovers you or I take.'

He was going to the door! 'Evan, I——' She half sat up. 'There's no one else. It's you——' *It's you I love* .... If she had finished the sentence, he would have laughed.

'If it's personal cash flow you're worried about, my bank accounts are yours. What more can I say to set your mind at rest?'

'Oh Evan, I——' She sat up and her arms came out.

His eyes gleamed and he put down his case. He stood beside the bed, looking down. 'Sexual deprivation—already? Good grief, Francesca, it's barely an hour since we——'

His arms were round her, holding her so that her head went back, her lips parted, her body shuddered under his possessive grip. Her throat yelped as his teeth nipped the swollen tips of her breasts, her breath came in gasps, moans escaped as his mouth took hers over and probed and thrust and brushed against her inner cheeks.

Her jaw throbbed when he let her go, her arms hung limp and empty. He straightened his jacket and adjusted his tie. 'That should keep you going for an hour or two,' he commented cynically, 'until he— whoever he may be—arrives.' He retrieved his suitcase.

'Evan, I told you, there's no one——' But he had gone.

Fran sank back against the pillows, her overstrung nerves at shrieking point at being so deeply aroused, yet so contemptuously discarded. The soreness and the bruising still troubled her, but she knew that the injuries had been relatively light and would not prevent her from getting dressed and even going out, if she wanted.

Going out—the words struck a chord, brought back memories of snow and skis and—*Johnny Black*. No, she reproached herself, it was wrong of her mind to bring that non-existent person back to life. He was nowhere, no one, a mere invention of her imagination.

Jerking her thoughts back to the present, she

formed a plan—only to hear a key in the door. Her pulses came back to invigorating life. Evan had returned, had only pretended to go away, as he had done at the chalet!

'Darling,' the silky feminine voice drifted through from the entrance lobby, 'you called me to come to you. Well, darling, I'm here?' The words rose in a question.

There were a few moments of silence, then the slender, emerald green clad figure appeared in the doorway to the bedroom. 'Oh, Mrs Dowd.' The words dropped like a graph to a new low. A false brightness lifted in her voice. 'Where have you hidden him? He called me to come over here. There's a job to do, he said. He wanted me here for a couple of days. To look after someone, he said. He didn't explain, but I knew what he meant—to come back to him, to look after *him*. In the ways he knows I can "look after" him. You should know,' she added unnecessarily, 'you've slept with him, too.'

Someone to 'look after'—Fran sat up dragging the bedclothes with her. Evan had been thoughtful for her after all. He had asked Willa to come to stay until she, Fran, had recovered completely. While the evidence of his consideration soothed her just a little, the situation did not please her at all.

Why had he sent for Willa, of all people, the person he must have known she least wanted to have as a companion no matter how temporary her stay. And had he really thought that 'other man' he had talked about would have come, knowing there was a third person in the place, an onlooker—a *witness*?

Was that it? she wondered, staring at her unwanted guest as she glanced, well-pleased, at her own reflection in the dressing-table mirror. Had he consulted a lawyer, wanting evidence of unfaithfulness, having eventual divorce in mind?

Fran reached for her dressing-gown and pulled it on, tying it.

'Evan's gone to the United States,' she said to the neat and tapered back which was towards her.

Willa turned as though an invisible hand had spun her. 'He has? Without me? You're fooling.' She watched unbelieving as Fran shook her head. 'Oh no.' She held her throat. 'But that must have been what he meant. That I should go with him—a job to do, he said. He's got a job for me? In the States?' Her eyes shone, her hands ran down her own shape as if checking its state of readiness for such a modelling job as America could offer her.

How could anyone, Fran mused, fool themselves as Willa was doing, misinterpreting words to suit her own needs, inventing a situation and putting themselves into it in a completely mistaken context.

'I don't think he meant that,' Fran hazarded, but doubted if anything she might say to dissuade the woman would register on her mind. She discovered she was right when Willa asked,

'What's his address over there? I must join him at once.'

With complete truth, Fran was able to answer, 'I'm sorry but I've no idea. He didn't give me any information. Except that he was catching a plane. From Frankfurt. Oh yes, to New York.'

Willa snapped her fingers. 'New York. Now, I can guess where he'll stay. Where we stayed before.'

'You've been with him there?' Her voice was small and, she couldn't help it, with the merest trace of envy.

'Oh, dozens, hundreds of times. Now,' she frowned at Fran, 'you'll be okay? Evan said you had to stay in bed to get over your accident. You were lucky, weren't you? Or did you arrange the near-accident deliberately, to get Evan's sympathy?'

The twist of Willa's mood took Fran by surprise, putting her on the defensive. 'It was a complete accident. I'd have had to be in a bad way to have tried to get run over.'

'I thought you were in a state. I saw your face. I also know your secret.' She smiled at the quick flush that invaded Fran's cheeks. 'But you've lost the game. To me. I'm going to get him back.'

'You might get as far as living with him,' Fran retaliated, keeping surprisingly cool, 'but he'll never legalise it. We married on condition that we stay that way, come what may, or whoever may—other women for Evan, other men for me.'

Willa's smile was slow and knowing. 'Don't bet your last shilling on it, will you? I know that man better than you do.'

Fran looked at the large, square-shaped modern clock on the sideboard. She had to get rid of Willa Hemming somehow and had an inspiration. 'If you hurry, really hurry, you might just catch Evan as he boards his plane.' It was a long shot, but to her astonishment, it worked.

'You know, you may be right.' Willa's eyes brightened. 'Thanks for the tip. Maybe you aren't so bad after all. But where that man's concerned, I've got no scruples. Sorry, *Mrs Dowd*. 'Bye.' She was out of the door before it had fully opened. It slammed shut and Fran's head dropped. The sound seemed so final.

CHAPTER NINE

I can't stay here. The words rang in Fran's mind. Hurrying as though she might be discovered any moment, she ran to the bathroom and showered, gasping as the water stung her grazed skin.

Ringing the airport, she booked a flight to London late that afternoon. Then she thumbed through the directory, running down the long list of people who had Dietmar Müller's name and, she discovered to her dismay, his initial.

The first three numbers she tried were wrong. The fourth connection was to someone who had a few words of English, the fifth spoke the language fluently and said he actually knew Dietmar Müller and gave her the correct number. Relieved, she thanked him profusely.

'Müller.' The name bounced off her ear, and she wondered whether she had indeed found the right connection this time. When the man had listened to her rather halting explanation for ringing, he laughed and said, 'Yes, this is Dietmar. You have had trouble finding me? Our name is like the very large number of Smiths in your telephone directories. Now, you wish me after all to take you and the fashion model around in my car?'

'Thank you, but not this time.' She explained about her accident. 'It was minor, luckily. My instinct for self-preservation must be very strong,' she joked, then thought, as a picture of Evan flashed into her mind, Is it?

Dietmar was very conerned and asked her how he could help her.

'Evan has had to go overseas,' she explained, 'and I have a flight back to Britain this afternoon.'

'So you are leaving? But you will, I hope, be back soon. Now, you have no transport—you see, I remember that—so I will give you a lift to Frankfurt. Yes?'

'Yes, please, Dietmar, and thank you very much.'

He laughed at her gratitude and asked, 'Will you please allow me to take you to a restaurant for your lunch?'

It would mean, Fran thought, that I would have someone to talk to and agreed at once.

'Shall we say one o'clock?' he suggested.

'Fine,' she said and rang off.

The rest of the morning Fran spent re-packing her belongings and tidying the apartment. She did not know if she would ever see it again. Nor could she see a way into the future for her marriage to Evan. Her depth of feeling for him frightened her.

Dietmar spent all of lunchtime talking about Sabina. Fran wished Evan had been there to hear him; it would have proved her point beyond doubt—that her acquaintance with Dietmar was based on friendship and nothing else.

This time, Dietmar had good reason for his non-stop praise—Sabina had at last agreed to resume their relationship. Not only that, they had become engaged and had a wedding date in mind.

'Will you tell Evan?' Fran asked in a tone that was not simply a question but a request.

'I will tell him. Of course.' Dietmar sounded puzzled.

Poor man, he doesn't know, Fran thought, that there's been more than a business acquaintance between his fiancée and my husband.

As she left him in the airport lounge to catch her

flight, Dietmar drew her to him and kissed her. 'You do not object?' he asked. 'Here we are not usually so demonstrative, but it has been so good to know you. I am sure Evan would not mind, even if he were here.'

Fran smiled secretly, knowing Evan's curiously forceful feelings on the subject. The flight path crossed the river Rhine. Gazing down, Fran saw specks that were barges and cruising ships; while wooded slopes gave way to fruitful vineyards and hid mysterious castles.

Her mind sped back to the days of the so-called honeymoon. Closing her eyes, she saw cobbled roads and pavements, town squares where artists sat painting near to spurting fountains; street cafés and aproned waiters; wide-flung shutters overlooking narrow roads where voices rose to drift through opened windows over the sound of chiming bells . . .

And all the time Evan had been beside her, arm around her waist or his hand entwined with hers. His lips had rarely been far away, whether whispering in her ear or seeking hers out and linking them both in a kiss.

'Fasten your seat belts.' The voice, joined by the flashing lights, drew her back from the past and plunged her simultaneously into the descent to earth and reality.

There was a 'phone call next morning. 'Who's that?' Fran asked. 'Ralph? Yes, I'm back from Germany. Evan's not here, he's in America. You guessed that? Why?'

Fran had returned to Evan's London house, but had no intention of remaining there. It would be the first place he would make for on his return. Until she had learned to live without him, she did not want to take the risk of being in physical contact with him again.

Ralph answered, 'He asked me to fly to Frankfurt to take his place in negotiations with the Müller family. He told me to stay at the apartment and that I'd find you there. I was convinced I'd misheard him, because I was sure you'd be going with him, if nothing else to see the fashions across the Atlantic. So I thought I'd better check with the London house first.'

Once again, Fran marvelled at the way Evan had shown consideration for her, making sure someone would be around to look after her in his absence. What did that reveal? she wondered, feeling a faint glow of hope around her heart. That he had some kind of feeling for her? More likely, a stirring guilt. It also told her something else—that he had intended all along to invite Willa to join him in New York, but had delayed doing so until Ralph had gone to the apartment to take her place.

'I'm glad you checked,' she told him, 'I had an accident, it was a slight one. A car hit me.' There was an intake of breath from the other end. 'Cuts and bruises, that's all. Someone gave me a lift to the airport yesterday. I took a taxi back here, so the journey wasn't difficult.' A thought occurred to her, a way of avoiding meeting Evan when he came back.

'If you're going away for a few days——'

'Couple of weeks, Evan said.'

Better still, Fran thought. 'Would you mind if I stayed at your place? I could look after it for you——'

'Why not stay where you are? It's your home now, after all.' Was there the merest trace of bitterness in the statement?

'It's—it's difficult to explain, Ralph. You know, a long story.'

'It's not over already, is it? I'd have thought Evan would have made more of an effort this time to make his marriage last.'

It was a question, she realised, to which she did not have to supply an answer. 'If you'd rather I didn't come,' she began, but Ralph broke in,

'I didn't say that. The flat's yours all the time I'm away. I believe——' there was a small pause, 'you still have a key to the place?'

'Sorry I forgot to return it, Ralph.'

'That's okay.' He sounded cheerful again. 'Leave it on a hook when you go, will you?'

'I'll be round in the morning,' she told him and rang off.

The house had never seemed so large as it did to Fran that day. In Evan's absence abroad, it had remained empty, although it had been cleaned and aired daily. In her wanderings around the rooms, she tried but did not once succeed in feeling she belonged there, nor that its splendours were legally hers to share. The explanation was simple, she told herself. Its owner, although on paper her husband, was not truly hers to share, either. He was his own man, controlling his own destiny regardless of all others, and no one, certainly no woman, Fran reflected sadly, would make him diverge from whatever course he had set himself.

During the afternoon, the telephone rang again. Fran's nerves jangled at the sound and she realised how on edge she had grown. Was it Ralph again, this time telling her she couldn't stay in his flat after all? Or was it a transatlantic call—Evan asking her what she was doing there? Or telling her that Willa and he were joining up again? But that the marriage would go on and on ... It won't be threatened, he'd said, no matter how many extra-marital affairs we each have.

'Fran here,' she said, then wondered if the caller could hear. It was plain the caller could not.

'Who is that?' The voice was surely Evan's? Incisive, a little impatient?

'This——' she moistened her lips, 'is Fran, Francesca.'

'Ah. So Evan will not be far away.' Fran's heartbeats slowed.

'Sir Lionel. No, Evan's not here. He's in the United States.'

'So,' the caller paused to consider, 'why are you not with him?' How, Fran thought, could she talk herself out of this one? Should she even try? 'I rang expecting no reply,' Evan's father went on, 'last I heard you were both at Evan's apartment in Germany, but I thought I'd better check.'

'Evan had to leave the negotiations,' Fran explained. 'Ralph's taking his place. I—well, I had work to come back to, Sir Lionel.'

'I see.' Fran wondered if he did. 'Er——' Sir Lionel's hesitation was uncharacteristic. 'Could you, at some not too distant date, manage to address me less formally? Father, maybe? Or even Lionel?'

Fran's smile was shaky as she stared unseeingly at the spray of tall, dried grasses across the hall. Call this distinguished man Father? She pressed her lips together. There could be no substitute for her own, who did not want to know her. And Lionel? The familiarity was not, in the circumstances and in her present state of mind, permissible.

'Could I—er—could I come back to you on that? In—in a few months? A few years?'

'Ah.' The syllable came out again as immediate comprehension dawned. She thought, I like this man who's my father-in-law, I like his quickness, his understanding. If only his son had inherited just a small percentage of it . . .

'Things,' he was saying, 'are a little difficult? You're missing that essential ingredient from the marriage recipe? The one you were so certain you could do without?'

'Love? Yes,' she admitted slowly and with an honesty that surprised herself, 'I'm missing it.'

'What, my dear, of your decision never to love a man. How has that fared in your early experience of marriage?'

'As a decision, it was untenable.'

'You're surprisingly truthful. Shall I tell you something?' He paused, though not for an answer, since nothing was plainly going to stop him. 'That day I left you—your wedding day, in fact—I saw something in your face that made me a happier man. I saw love. You may not have been aware of it yourself, and I'm certain that Evan was not.'

'I didn't know myself then,' she commented thoughtfully. I did, she thought, right from the beginning, but I refused to acknowledge it. 'And since the day I discovered I was in——' she corrected herself hastily, 'felt affection for him, I've pretended otherwise.'

'You haven't told him? Not at any time, nor any place?'

There was a gentle laughter in the deep voice that had Fran blushing. 'Nor any place,' she confirmed. 'Even if I—I had,' she paused to still the sudden falter, 'he would have dismissed it as a result of what we were d——' Embarrassed, she corrected herself again, 'arising from the circumstances prevailing at the time.'

This time the laughter was louder, the amusement real. 'I told Evan the first time I met you how fussy you were about the correct word, the apt expression.'

It's shyness, she could have told him, at discussing such a personal subject but she laughed with him at herself.

'So,' he altered his tone, 'Evan's in the States. When is he due back?'

If only she could have told him! 'I don't know, Sir Lionel,' was all she said, but her tone said much more. She added, then regretted it immediately, 'He's not alone. Willa, his ex-wife, is with him.'

There was a telling silence. 'You're sure of this?'

'Quite sure,' and she told him how she knew.

A sharp, impatient sigh brushed her ear. 'Well, goodbye, my dear,' said Sir Lionel and rang off.

That evening, Fran gave her mind some work to do. Well into the dark hours she sorted through her papers, thinking through the weeks ahead to the fashion features the magazine would carry. In the morning, she added a few more items to her already packed cases and made her way to Ralph's apartment a few miles distant.

She used the key and entered, lifting in her luggage. There was music playing and a voice talking over it. Ralph was seated at the breakfast bar watching television.

Surprised, he swung round, seeing her surprise at discovering him there.

'My flight's this afternoon,' he explained. This had not occurred to her, having assumed he would have left by now. 'But it doesn't matter. Make yourself at home. You're not a stranger here.'

Peering at him, she thought, There's no bitterness, nor sarcasm. Has he finally reconciled himself to my marriage to his stepbrother?

'I still don't know why you've come here,' he added, 'but that doesn't matter, either. It's your business.' Gladly, silently, she agreed with him.

'Which room?' she called over the background noise.

'Mine,' he answered. 'The other bedroom's full to the ceiling with rubbish.'

Putting her cases down, she shook her head at the

untidy bedclothes and the masculine chaos around the room, then she started stripping the bed. The telephone on the bedside table rang. Fran stared at it, waiting for Ralph to answer its call.

'Get it for me, Fran, will you?' His voice came from the distance. 'Won't be a minute.'

Lifting the 'phone, she held it to her ear, saying nothing.

'Ralph?' The voice was incisive and slightly impatient.

She recognised it this time. 'Sir Lionel? Ralph won't be a moment. He's just had breakfast and he's——'

Her body went cold, her breath froze in her throat. Oh yes, she told herself furiously, I recognise that voice, don't I? *And it's not Sir Lionel Dowd's!*

There was a prolonged, crackling pause. Then the words hit her, like hurled boulders all the way across the Atlantic. 'You hypocritical, double-dealing little bitch!' The 'phone was rammed down, all contact cut.

It was work that kept her going over the following days. Ralph had rung from Germany to say his return to London was delayed by a week and she could stay on at his place if she wished. Gladly she did so, more afraid than ever of meeting Evan face to face.

From the start of their acquaintance, he'd said keep away from Ralph. Now he thought—was obviously convinced—that she had run back to him. But if it had been Dietmar he had thought she had gone with, or any other man, would his reaction have been the same?

That, she told herself, was something she would never know. There was nothing now to cause him to give up Willa. This marriage contract she, Fran, had made with him would stand—he'd said so repeatedly—while their respective affairs came and went.

Which meant, she went on thinking, that even if she denied that there was anything between herself and Ralph, and even if Evan believed it, it would make no difference to their future. They would still live out their marriage separately, each going his or her own way. And since there wasn't another man on earth she wanted to be with, her way would be a very lonely one. And that, she reasoned swallowing the tears, brings me full circle to my mother's position.

She shook her head, staring blindly at her wedding ring, thinking, Why do we never learn from mistakes, either other people's or even our own? I thought I had, I really did, she told herself, I was sure my reason had the upper hand, that my emotions had been locked away and the key lost for ever. What I didn't know, she reflected, was that emotions could be so strong they could burst through the toughest barrier, the strongest prison wall.

One morning, two personal letters were handed to her as she sat at her desk. Recognising her mother's handwriting, she tore the top one open eagerly. It had been months since she had heard from her parents, even though she had written to them separately and told them of her marriage. It had hurt her deeply that they had shown so little interest in her affairs they had not even written asking the identity of the man she had married.

'My dear Fran,' her mother had written, 'please forgive me for being so unmother-like and not writing to say how pleased I was to hear of your marriage. *This goes for your father, too.*' This last had been heavily underlined.

Fran frowned, then smiled, her brow clearing in hope.

'Yes, we have got together again. Well, under one roof, anyway. We found that although we could not live happily together, we couldn't live happily apart, either. So we share the house—the one we lived in as a family and which your father kept on—and meet for meals, then go our own ways.'

Fran read the closely-written paragraph through again, having been too overjoyed to read it carefully the first time.

'One day,' her mother went on, 'it may become a real marriage again. Yes, dear, it is possible, even at your father's and my great ages (!) to have a real marriage. You're so young you may not believe this but it's true. But at present, we have decided to be friends, sharing friends, warm friends. And that is nice, very nice. When will we meet your handsome husband? He's sure to be handsome, no matter what shape his face might be. Love does wonders to the lover's eyes! Did you realise your mother was, after all, a romantic? Our combined love, Mother and Father.' They had each signed the letter.

For some time, Fran dreamed, the pleasure in her heart spilling over and warming her through, filling her eyes with tears of relief and a long-forgotten happiness.

Then she thought of her own fragmented marriage, a split into moments of rapture and days of despair. Nor, looking ahead, could she see a different and more hopeful way ahead. Abstractedly, she took up the second letter and turned it over, studying the typewritten address, the name of Mrs Fran Dowd, followed by her position on the magazine and its name, nothing else. It was stamped, yet it had not been franked. Had it been delivered by hand?

'Fran,' it said, 'I want to see you again. I have something to talk over. It concerns ourselves. Meet me at the Dowd chalet, three days' time. E.D.'

With shaking hands, she folded the letter, then

flipped it open. Three days from when? It was dated the day before, that day being Wednesday. She had just over one day in which to rearrange her appointments, rethink her work schedule, book a flight—and two days in which to worry herself to a standstill wondering just what it was Evan wanted to talk about. After the way their 'phone conversation—if that was what it had been—had ended, it could be anything, anything at all.

CHAPTER TEN

ALL the way to the chalet in Switzerland, Fran spent trying to analyse the contents of the note which Evan had sent her. She had learnt it by heart.

He wanted to see her again ... something to talk about ... The fact that he wanted to see her at all, no matter where the meeting place might be, gave her tremendous hope.

It was only when she opened the chalet door and entered the large, echoing building that doubts began to assail her. It was like a second showing of a film, as though the questions she had asked herself the first time she had gone to the chalet—why am I here, should I have come?—still hung in the air waiting to be answered all over again.

It was late morning but Evan had not arrived, that much was certain. There was no sound, no sign of occupation. No partly used milk in the fridge, no untidy bedroom. Nor was there a tough-hewn, dark-haired man filling the place with his dynamism, his body spelling out security, reliability, his face outlined with strength, and shaded in with ruthlessness tempered here and there with mercy and a lurking laughter.

A wave of longing impelled her to the window and her sweeping, searching eyes saw that the winter snow had gone, giving place to an all-enveloping greenness. The mountains climbed towards the deeply blue sky, trees trod up steep slopes, lifting themselves straight and tall, as if competing with each other to attain the record height.

It was summertime at a winter sports resort and the season's finery, the best that Nature could offer, warmed the heart. It was Fran's heart that changed in beat from a low drumming to a race against time. Her eyes had picked up a moving figure down there among the chalets' sloping roofs and flower-decked balconies.

He was climbing the hill, head down, backpack swinging from his hand; booted feet, sure in their hold and their knowledge of the terrain, thumping upward. There was no hurry in his bearing, no head lifted in anticipation, only a dogged pounding of the green turf and rock-hard path towards his destination.

Fran glanced down at herself, wishing she had packed a glamorous dress, a clinging Willa-type gown that shimmered and flowed and had 'I'm soft and feminine, try me' written in invisible letters across it.

Instead, she had showered and chosen a pink blouse and white slacks, fixing a white-beaded necklace around her throat, hurrying in case Evan came before she was ready.

As she watched him approach, her thoughts took her to the door, flinging it wide and waiting, arms spread to wrap around him. But her feet did not move and a sudden panic put her hand to her throat, while her other arm pressed defensively against her waist.

The door to the chalet swung open. Fran's heart raced and jumped. Her face grew warm, her thick brown hair fell to her shoulders and, as she turned from the window, swung wide to settle in strands, some partly covering her face.

She did not push them away. She felt a need for their protection and when she saw the face of the man who stood staring at her, she knew why.

'You?' his hard lips said, twisting bitterly. 'What the hell are you doing here?' He did not speak in pleased surprise, nor even in expectation, but with a snarling anger. 'Have I disrupted your plans again like the first time we met here? Who's the secret assignation with this time—no, don't tell me, I'll take a guess. My stepbrother Ralph. Who else since I know for a fact that you've spent all your nights with him since my departure for the U.S.'

Fran shook her head. 'You don't know anything "for a fact", Evan.'

He dropped the backpack and peeled the jacket from his shoulders.

'So who was it I spoke to the other day when I called his flat? Who was it who thought I was *Sir Lionel*?' He kicked the backpack aside. 'Who told me, oh so cosily, that Ralph wouldn't be a minute, he'd just had breakfast and, I've no doubt you were going to add, but stopped yourself in time that he hadn't yet recovered from your exhausting night together.' He was standing over her now, arms folded, feet apart, menace in every line of him.

'You know it was me on the 'phone, Evan,' she rallied in the face of his belligerence, 'but what you don't know and probably wouldn't accept as the truth if I told you, was that I'd only just arrived there——'

'Why?'

'To—to——' she knew what she was going to say would incriminate herself just as badly in his eyes, 'to stay there, that's why.'

'When you had a perfectly good home to live in of your own? No cancel that.' His mouth resumed its bitter line. 'Of course, my stepbrother was the attraction.'

'No, no, you're wrong.' How could she tell him, 'I was afraid of meeting you there until I'd learned to live without you'? 'It's not my home,' she said at last. 'It never has been and,' her head lifted bravely, 'never will be, will it. After all,' she threw at him, 'where would you carry on all those extra-marital affairs of yours if I were around the place?'

His hands clamped on each side of her head, forcing it back so that she had to gaze into his anger-darkened eyes. 'And, by the same token, where will you conduct yours if I'm around? It's not only Ralph, is it? It's Dietmar, too. And there are others, aren't there?'

Fran whispered, her throat dry, her head beginning to ache, 'What others?'

'There's Andy, there's Mike, there's Dave, all Dowd Wideworld employees.'

The trembling tip of her tongue ran round her cracked lips. 'How—how do you know them?' Then she heard her own question and realised that she had unintentionally confirmed his allegations of involvement with those young men.

He jerked his hands from her. 'I made it my business.' He slipped his fingers under his belt. 'You were surrounded by them that first day I ever saw you.'

'At the Wideworld convention?'

'Where else? I'd seen a photo of you in Ralph's possession, had his description of you—which, I might add, fell short of the real thing—and managed, by mingling, to spot you among all the other Dowd employees. When I saw you giving them the green light all round, I knew that for you any man would do and that Ralph would have to be physically prevented from making a fool of himself over you. So I sent him to Germany.'

'You were at that conference? But I was told you had a pressing appointment elsewhere.'

'I did. With you, here at the chalet.'

'But you arrived before me.'

'I left the convention before you. I knew the way. You didn't. I had fast transport. You didn't.'

'So now I know,' she pushed the strands of hair aside, revealing her flushed, unhappy face, 'why you really married me—to keep me away from Ralph.'

'Did I?' His face was cold, his eyes like glittering ice. 'I told you why, when I proposed. I wanted to have a legal woman in my life. In other words, a wife. Also,' he went on brutally, 'I wanted a marriage without the responsibility of loving or being loved. And,' he clicked his fingers in her wan face, 'I got it.'

'You call love a *responsibility*?' she cried. 'I never realised how cold and—and cruel your nature really is.'

'It took you a long time to learn.' His jaw hardened. He turned away. 'There's nothing more to say.'

'But you wanted to see me here.' Her voice seemed to come from far away. He swung back. 'I did? I can't recall, after our telephone conversation, ever wanting to see you again.'

'You sent me a note.'

'I sent you no note.' His eyes narrowed. 'Got it with you? No? Who signed it?'

'You did. It was stamped and in an envelope. It was quite plain you had——' Then she visualised it. There had been no signature, only typed initials. The realisation showed in her face.

'I'm glad you acknowledge I'm right. How could I have sent the letter from New York bearing a British stamp?'

She shook her head. 'I didn't think about that. All I was concerned with was that you wanted to see me——'

'Would I have gone to the trouble of getting you to come here? Wouldn't I have gone to the London house?' His eyes flickered. 'Correction, contacted Ralph's flat—you would have been there, wouldn't you?'

What else could she do, she thought, but nod? At each of his questions her heart had descended another step towards despair.

'What did you expect when we met,' his sarcastic tone cut into her, 'a grand reconciliation scene?' He distanced himself, looking her over. 'You're out of date. Relationships these days are based on shifting sand. Love comes, love goes. The tide flows in and each time it goes out, it takes away a bit, then a bit more of the initial feeling, until nothing's left. Not even the attraction.' His look drove into her, making her sway with inner pain. He could not have made his meaning more clear.

Her shoulders drooped and she turned to go back to the bedroom she had used the first time she had visited the place.

'When is he coming?'

Fran turned. 'When's who coming?' The penny dropped. 'No one's coming.'

'That I do not believe. You invent a letter which you said I sent you, making that an excuse for a visit here——'

'The letter exists,' she replied. 'I don't know who sent it but if I had it with me I could show it to you.' She went on her way knowing that she still had not convinced him.

She was running a comb through her hair when he appeared in the bedroom doorway. He propped himself against it and just watched. She felt the pull of him as if he had physically thrown a rope around her and was tugging her towards him. Was he doing it on purpose?

Angrily, she turned round and saw the mocking smile. 'So in the absence of any other man, you're making yourself attractive for me.' He pushed himself from the door and approached her slowly. 'That's okay. I'll oblige any time where you're concerned, my dove,' his teeth snapped together and he dragged her against him by the shoulders, 'any time at all.' Her head went back—it could not go forward because his chest was a wall in front of it—and his gaze searched hers as if he were drawing her into him. 'My loins are responding to your physical presence just as they always did. Absence from you is spicing my needs and they won't let me rest until I've had you. Take off your things before I tear them off.' He pushed her away and with lowered lids watched her frightened indecision. 'You're afraid of my hunger? Haven't ever seen a starving animal tear at its food?'

Slowly, she did as he had ordered. Just as slowly, he removed his checked shirt and bunched it, throwing it across the room. The rest of his clothing followed and she felt the sweeping excitement of the total touch of him, all down her throbbing body.

'You come alive,' he said, his lips rough against her tender skin, 'when I take you next to me. Your eyes shine,' he lifted his head and looked into them, 'and I could—almost—believe there was feeling there. But,' he forced his leg through hers, 'even if there is, it's as false as a mirage in a desert.'

He tipped her backwards until she fell to the carpet and he went with her. He did not take her to the bed. His lips sought her hardened breasts, his fingers twined painfully in her long tangled hair. His hands were unsparing on her slender body and when at last he took her, the action was that of a man seeking, not a joyful coming together, but revenge.

For a long time, he kept her there, letting her feel the weight of him. There was a crying pain inside her, and it had nothing to do with the pressure of his body. It was the way he had treated her that tore at her heart, his contemptuous taking of her, merely to assuage his masculine appetite.

He moved away at last and she curled into herself, shivering, on the bedside rug. A few moments later, she heard the water running, but there was no loud singing voice over the sound. Johnny Black had, indeed, gone for ever.

'Why did you come here?' Fran asked, complimenting herself on the veneer of poise she had managed to assume. They had eaten lunch which Fran had cooked and now, on low chairs near the window, drank their coffee.

All the time since they had come together, Evan had remained aloof and self-contained. It was almost, Fran thought with deep sadness, as though they had not even touched, let alone made love.

Now she knew what it was really like to be intimate without emotion, without heart. Afterwards, there was nothing, no reaching out to the other, no transformation of the passion aroused into a holding of hands, a desire to touch and keep touching, renewing the contact, reliving the joy.

Evan stretched out his long legs and put back his head. 'I came for a walking holiday, a short break before resuming my business commitments.'

It was something she would have loved to do, to go walking at his side over these hills and mountains. 'Alone?' she heard herself ask, then told herself she should have expected the sardonic look that came her way.

'Not alone,' he stated blandly. 'With friends. Yes,' at her surprised look, 'I have plenty of friends among this crowd.'

'The beautiful people.' She could not resist the taunt.

'Of which you're implying, I'm one?'

She had not thought so, but she found herself agreeing. 'And your ex-wife. You were made for each other. Yet you had to marry me to discover it.'

'I've discovered it, have I?'

'You took her with you to America. I've no doubt at all that you didn't say "no" whenever she beckoned.'

He sent her a speaking glance that told her nothing and rose in a leisurely manner. There was a glint of amusement in his eyes as he bent over her, lifting her chin and placing a careless kiss on her lips. 'You'll never know, will you?' he tormented softly and left her.

When he returned, he was dressed for walking and her heart took a dive again. Had he meant what he said about a walking holiday? But there was no sign of his backpack.

'Will you be away long?' she asked, standing up and hugging herself to suppress a shiver that threatened. Was all her life going to be like this—a withdrawing of her real self into hiding whenever they met? Restraining her feelings every time he made love to her, pretending a sophisticated boredom when it was over? When all she really wanted to do was to throw her arms around him and whisper, I love you. Let's make love again?

'Why?' His lip curled. 'You want to know how long you've got with your lover? Where's he staying? At one of the hotels down in the town?'

Something tore free inside her and she cried, 'There isn't a "he", I don't have a lover. He exists in your mind, nowhere else! Don't you understand? No,' she didn't wait for an answer, 'you don't, you won't ever, because you don't want to. You want to be free to have woman after woman. You as good as told me the day you proposed. Here,' her anguished eyes swept round, 'in this chalet. Well, you can feel free, because I'm going—going out.'

'Where?' he asked coldly, totally unmoved by her words.

'I don't know. Somewhere,' she threw a glance outside, 'anywhere, where I can get away, think—be myself. Not chained to you anymore.' Her eyes went over him hungrily, loving his strength, his whipcord muscularity, yet she made the glance into a look of scorn. 'I hate being your wife. I want my freedom, do you hear?'

'The condition of our marriage,' he rapped out, 'was that you could have that freedom—within the marriage. I could have similar freedom, again inside the marriage. So go ahead, take it. Do what you like with it. Go and meet your lover. *But the marriage stands.*' He turned and strode out.

There was bustle and movement everywhere as Fran made her way into the town. Sunlight heightened the colour of the flowers that overflowed from balconies, danced over canopies and threw shadows on to the brightly-dressed passers-by.

They gazed about them, their eyes pleased with what the townsfolk had to offer, with the souvenir shops, the stores that sold skiing equipment along with dreams of the snowbound sparkling season to come.

Fran recognised the shop to which Evan had taken her to buy clothes for her first attempts at skiing. Bittersweet memories tore at her thoughts, making her close her eyes. A shop window offered a moment's seclusion. Voices approached and one in particular had her listening. She would know it anywhere, a man's voice, deep and resonant, full of authority—and laughter.

A woman was talking now, but the conversation

seemed to be in French. The pace of it was too fast for her halting knowledge of the language to get even the gist of it. Opening her eyes, yet not turning around, she saw the reflected images go past.

Evan's was unmistakable, even if he had not been wearing the loose jacket and dark pants in which he had left the chalet. The woman was tall, slim and blonde. It only took a second for Fran to recognise the graceful bearing, the flowing walk. Willa Hemming was there again, and Evan had sought her out, pretending he had been joining 'friends'!

As soon as the reflections had passed, Fran crossed the road and looked quickly from left to right. Where should she go? Anywhere, she sought, to escape from the misery of dwelling on the knowledge that she had finally lost the battle for Evan's love. It had never been hers to fight for, she knew that now, because it had never been taken away from the woman he married first time round.

A sign caught her eye, directing tourists to the chairlift. In a few moments she was up the stairs and buying a ticket. The line of chairs moved continuously and as one came round, she gripped its swaying side and clambered in.

The view, as the chair rose higher, took her breath. Her mind soared, freed, for just a while from the unhappiness from which she was seeking to escape. Wide-roofed chalets, balconies alight with flowers, stretched way below in the valley that was unwinding beneath her. Green banks of trees clambered up the slopes, trying their best to reach the snow-capped summits which rose all around.

The chair neared the terminus and Fran turned to see a collection of buildings. People walked around, children darted here and there. A child ran past as Fran stepped out of the still-moving chair. She misjudged the distance to the ground and stumbled to her knees. A woman came over to help her and asked in French if she had hurt herself.

Fran managed to assure her that it was nothing and she would be fine and the woman left her. Finding a tissue, she dabbed at her knees. One was bruised, while the other was grazed and bleeding slightly. There was a kiosk beside the café and she limped to it, asking with miming actions if there was a plaster available. A packet was produced, for which Fran gratefully paid and she went into the café, ordering coffee. Having washed her hands, she applied a plaster and the soreness receded.

For some time she lingered over her coffee, staring out at the view, only half seeing it. Her worries, she told herself, might have been left down there in the valley, but they were waiting for her on her return. Restlessly, she got up and made for the viewing platform, lining up the mountain peaks with the engraved guide mounted on a pillar.

Everything was so green and summerlike, she found it impossible to imagine the whole panorama covered in deep snow, even though she had seen it like that only a few weeks earlier. Down there, she thought, everything looks so small. Are my worries in reality that small, too? Why can't I go on accepting this loveless marriage I have? After all, it was the last time I was here that I told Evan 'yes' to his proposal. It was what I wanted, wasn't it—no emotional entanglement? But, she argued, noticing the shadows climbing the slopes as the sun moved lower, I was a different person then.

Lingering in the souvenir shop, she bought one or two items, pushing them into her bag. After another coffee and a roll, she wandered outside and saw a board bearing a map of the area. There was, she discovered, a path down the hill.

In her pocket was a return ticket. The chair-lift was a quicker way down, but was it speed she wanted? It would only take her all the faster to the chalet, to an interminable evening of wondering and waiting, listening for Evan's return, not alone, but with his former wife.

Her feet moved impulsively towards the pathway and she did not check their progress. At first, her spirits soared. She stopped now and then to gaze at the view, inhale the pure air and take a short rest. These rests became a little longer each time and she became aware that her injured knee was aching. If only, she thought, I'd asked how long it usually took to walk down.

A sudden chill caught her, penetrating the thin jacket she had pulled on. She had not realised how cold it could become among the mountains when the sun dropped behind them.

Looking down, then upward, she knew that it was too late to turn back. The small amount of food she had eaten since lunch had done nothing to renew her energies. Her other leg was aching now, having had to take the weight the injured leg could not.

She sat down on the green slope just off the path and saw that the mountains' shadows were reaching down to cover the landscape with growing darkness. She was alone in a strange land and no one would know where to find her. She had not even told Evan where she was going. 'Somewhere, anywhere,' she had said. 'I want my freedom.' Well, I've got it, she thought, it's all around me. What am I going to do with it? She lay back, putting an arm across her eyes. What, she wondered helplessly, was that freedom going to do with her?

Awakening with a start, she looked around. The

darkness was rising all about her. She had not meant to sleep, it had crept up on her. She had been tired, she recognised, not just from the fall and the walk, but from everything that had gone before.

Listening intently, she hoped for the sound of voices, but heard only the great, enclosing silence. After a time, there was another sound—like someone walking, but it was too indistinct for her to be sure. It was, she decided, yet another mirage in the particular desert in which she was wandering. No one else, she knew, would come that way at that hour.

Then there came a shout, drawn out and echoing. *Frances-ca-a, Frances-s-ca!* Only one person in the world spoke her name like that. Her heart pounded, then bounded.

'*Evan!*' It was a feeble sound through a throat that was dry, lips that were parched. She tried to stand but there was a weakness in her limbs. He would go past in the darkness, he would miss her completely!

She covered her face with her hands and found dampness on them. They were being moved from her cheeks, a man was crouching, looking into her tear-filled eyes.

'What,' Evan said, 'is so upsetting about sitting on a mountainside in the sunset?'

'How—how did you know I was here?' she faltered.

'I asked at the top if anyone of your description had been seen around.' He straightened. 'They remembered you, but couldn't tell me much except that you'd bought a few things, although that at least established that you'd been up here.'

He slid his backpack to the ground. 'If you're not the craziest female I've ever come across!' He extracted a flask from the pack, unscrewed the top and poured, the aroma telling her it was coffee. 'I know these hills and mountains like I know the alphabet,' he went on. 'I've skiied on them, climbed on them, even slept on them. I took a guess, inspired as it turned out, that you might make for the chairlift. What I didn't guess was that you'd be foolish enough to attempt to walk down.'

'The path looked straightforward enough on that notice board up there.'

'Maybe,' he agreed, 'but not dressed as you are and at this time of day.'

The flask, as he moved it, knocked against her leg and she exclaimed, nursing it, 'Please be careful. It hurts.'

'Here, take this coffee. What's wrong with your leg?'

Fran explained what had happened. He shook his head. 'How many times since I've known you have you injured yourself?'

'I've lost count,' she answered, her tone flat. 'I can't help it if I'm accident prone.' And, she thought, in more ways than you'll ever know.

'So you admit it at last.' He poured more coffee and produced a packet of sandwiches.

Fran took the coffee. 'I'm not hungry, thanks,' she told him. 'Just guide me the rest of the way down this mountain and I'll get myself out of your life. Then you'll be free to get back to your ex-wife.'

'You'll eat this food if I have to force it down you.'

'Yes,' she retorted bitterly, 'you can force me in a— a lot of ways, can't you? Regardless of my wishes, my feelings——'

'When have feelings entered into our relationship?' She did not answer, aware that she had almost given herself away. 'Now, get this sandwich into you. You'll need the strength it gives. I'm not carrying you down. You'll do it under your own steam.'

'I'd refuse to let you carry me, even if you offered.' She chewed the sandwich uncaringly, staring down into the darkened valley.

Evan's face was lit by a residual glow from the sunset. She wanted to touch his cheeks, his chin, his mouth. She wanted his arms around her, reassuring her that, even though he did not love her, there was a place for her in his life, after all.

'What's this,' he asked, repacking the bag, 'about getting back to my ex-wife?'

'I saw you with her down there in the town. I'd know Willa anywhere. Tall and blonde and beautiful. You were both talking and laughing. If you're reconciled, don't let me stand in the way.'

'What were we saying?'

She lifted her shoulders, then they shivered. 'Don't know, couldn't hear. Couldn't understand.' She paused. 'You were speaking in French.'

He looked at her curiously. 'Willa can't speak a word of French.'

'Then,' her heart jumped again, 'who——?'

'A friend. I told you, I have a number in these parts.'

Not Willa! But the lift of her spirits was temporary. Another friend, she thought, another woman on his list. 'Extra-marital friend?'

'Most definitely outside marriage,' he remarked drily, then removed his jacket.

'Put this on.'

'No, thank you. You'll get cold.'

'Since when have you been so concerned about my well-being?' His sarcasm silenced her but she thought, I could have told him—since the moment we met. Why, she asked herself, don't I tell him I love him? *But that would end it all . . .*

His shoulders tautened his shirt, his arm muscles evident even through the fabric. He stood, and Fran's admiring glance followed him up. Even in the semi-darkness, she saw that he had the physique and litheness of a born skier. She wanted the strength of him to wrap around her and never let her go.

'I don't want to go down the hill!' The words took her by surprise, breaking free of her control.

His legs were rigid in front of her, apart, like a skier readying for take-off. Any moment, he would turn and go and she would know the end of their relationship had come. Why hadn't she stopped herself from speaking?

'Tell me more.' The clipped words came from above her head.

She strained through the increasing darkness trying to see his expression. It was impossible to glean anything from the shape of his face, but his voice had sounded almost angry.

I could tell him, she thought, if we go down there, I shall lose you in the crowd again. But hadn't she lost him already? Had she ever found him, his real, true self? Yes, she remembered, once, twice, maybe, the side of him she loved so much had made an appearance. For the sake of that part of this man, she would tell him, and take the consequences.

'There isn't really much to tell,' she said hesitantly. 'Except that I——' It was inevitable now. She took a throbbing breath. 'I love you.' There was such a long, dark silence, she added, stumblingly, 'But it doesn't matter. Don't let it trouble you. We—we can go on as before.' Still he said nothing. 'I've been the foolish one again, haven't I? One accident after another . . .' She moistened her lips. 'Now I've committed the worst calamity of all.' Her face tilted upwards, the tears ran down her cheeks.

Her voice thickened. 'You can go down to the valley now. You can find that woman you were with. The blonde . . . so many blondes in your life.' A strained laugh escaped. 'And I'm a brunette. Not your type at

all, am I? Never have been. It's why you felt it was
safe to marry me, I suppose. No danger of your ever
falling in love with me . . . No!'

He had reached down and jerked her upright, his
fingers biting into her arms.

'Let me go,' she cried. 'I knew you'd be angry, but I
told you it didn't matter.' A sudden fear put energy
into her limbs and she struggled fiercely.

Then she was hard against him, in the iron circle of
his arms. His mouth bore down on hers and she felt
his intrusion into its innermost corners. She tried to
gasp his name, but he would not allow her even that
freedom.

When he finally lifted his head, she hung limp in his
arms. Then he pulled her back to him and she heard
the rumble of his voice as he said, 'What the hell did
you think I was going to do with you—throw you
down the hill?'

'I didn't know,' she said, 'how could I? You seemed
so angry with me for saying what I did.'

He urged her down and pulled her to him, his arm
around her. 'Want to know why I was angry? Because
you hadn't told me before. I'd had a suspicion it might
be so, but there was Dietmar, plus Ralph for the
second time.'

'They were friends, no less, no more,' she answered,
straining to return to her place against him. He held
her away. 'Will you believe me when I tell you that
when Dietmar took me to the airport that day you left,
he told me that he and Sabina were engaged?'

'I'll believe you, because it's so easy to check. I
seem to remember some insinuating remark you made
about myself and that beautiful but very cool lady.'

'You gave her such a lot of attention.'

'I know I did, but then she was saying some very
interesting, not to say important things. Fascinating

things, like financial standing and overheads and projected sales figures.'

Fran smiled in the darkness and reached out a hand to discover whether Evan was smiling, too. 'That note I got, which I thought was from you——'

'I've worked out its origin. I imagine that you called me Sir Lionel on the 'phone that day because you'd been speaking to my father at some time?'

She nodded against his chest. 'I told him I loved you. He got it out of me.'

'Ah.' He shifted her into a more comfortable position against him. 'So he thought he would play Cupid and get us together here to work things out between us. He knew I was coming here for a short break.' He laughed. 'My hard-headed, soft-centred father. He must have badly wanted my marriage to you to succeed.'

'There's something else—you invited Willa to New York,' Fran accused.

'Oh, I did not. She delivered herself on my doorstep there. I'd intended her to take care of you.'

'Will you tell me why,' she walked her fingers up his chest, 'you were so anxious for me to give Willa a modelling job.'

'I will. Her husband was a compulsive spender and he just about wrecked the marriage. She tried leaving him but now he's promised to reform. She needs the money to pay off his debts so that they can start again. I found her a well-paid modelling job in the States, after which she's going back to him.'

'She kept saying that you and she were getting together again. You didn't deny it, did you?'

'It wasn't worth a denial. You should have known there wasn't the slightest chance of that. I meant everything I said about my relationship with her. She did put me against women—until I met my stepbrother's girlfriend.' He smiled briefly. 'Satisfied?'

'And I thought you were concerned about her because you were still in love with her and wanted her to succeed. You're quite, quite sure you're not?'

He left a small silence. His hold around her loosened as he said, 'Are *you* sure you didn't spend the night, prior to that morning I spoke to you on the phone, with my stepbrother, Ralph?'

She sprang away from him. 'No, I did not!'

'Right. Which makes us quits. You have my answer, be content with it.'

He got to his feet and Fran stood with him. He was back to the fringes of anger and she did not know how to handle him any more. He looked around in the near-darkness.

'It's too late to get down to the town. We'll wait until first light. Follow me,' he instructed, retrieving the backpack and striking across the line of the hill.

Fran did her best to keep up with him. Now and then he glanced back, but she felt her slowness irritated him. 'Evan,' she called at last, 'my knee's hurting. You go on.'

He came to an abrupt halt. 'What do you take me for?' he snapped and back-tracked, swinging the pack around him and out of the way. He lifted her and carried her until they came to a hut, its black shape stark on the hillside.

Evan opened the door and pushed in, lowering her and raking in his bag for a torch. Its beam swung round, picking up the shape of hay bales and sacks. A heavy smell hung on the air and Fran guessed the place was a store for animal feed. The floor was hard and straw-strewn and through the one small window the night sky sparkled in.

He put the torch down and gathered some hay into a

pile. 'Right,' he said, hands on hips, 'this is our bed.'
His sardonic smile flashed in the lightbeam. 'Ever
slept rough before? Well, you're starting right now.
It's okay,' as Fran's apprehensive gaze went around
the hut, 'no animals here to share it with us.'

'Evan, I——'

To her relief and gratitude, he understood at once.
'There's the great big empty world out there. Not a
soul in sight. Wash your hands in the dew.'

Closeness, she thought as she went out, intimacy—
they're so much more than merely making love.

'Evan,' she said again as she returned, 'I'm hungry.'

His head went back in the semi-darkness and his
laughter filled the small hut. 'It's what I love about
you,' he commented, opening his pack, 'a quick
adjustment to changed circumstances and bouncing
back after every misfortune.'

She crouched down and deliberately stared into his
face. 'Just wanted to see,' she explained, 'if I could
detect any sarcasm.' He smiled down at her with such
uncharacteristic sweetness, she thought her heart
would melt. It must, she concluded, have been a trick
of the half light. Munching the sandwich Evan had
given her, she said, 'Is that all you love about me?'

She heard the question as it hung on the air and
added hastily, 'Don't answer that. Put it down to the
very unusual circumstances.'

'Is that how I'm supposed to explain away your
confession back there on the hill—that you love me?'

Now is my chance, she thought, to retract that
statement. Because it had been the truth, and because
she could not judge his mood, she answered, 'Explain
it how you like.'

He repacked the backpack and stretched out on the
bed of straw, cushioning his head with his arms. The
torch was on at his side. A taunting smile challenged

her to join him. Since there was no way of escaping the inevitable, she lowered herself beside him. She hugged her knees and waited. She looked around, her eyes delving into the dark shadows.

'Put out the light.' The words came softly from beside her.

Obeying, she reached over, pressing against him as she did so and clicked the switch. She felt his frame rising and falling with each breath. For a moment, she lingered, reluctant to break contact. Still he did not respond.

'Evan,' she whispered into the darkness, 'it's true what I told you. I do love you.' She settled beside him. 'I'm sorry I've broken the conditions of our marriage. But as I said,' her voice was smaller now, 'don't let it worry——'

There was a small sound, growing louder, like a man singing. '*When a woman lies beside a man and offers him love for money,*' the words came teasingly out of the darkness, '*she lies with her eyes, she lies with her lips . . .*'

Fran held her breath.

'*She lies with her sighs, she lies with her hips . . .*' went the song.

'Johnny,' she cried, 'Johnny Black! That's the side of you I fell in love with, the part of you I thought I'd never see again.'

Hands came out and hauled her round and on to him, wrapping about her and exerting such pressure that all of her softness was moulded against the angles of his hardness and she gasped with laughter.

Her face was imprisoned between two wide palms and he said, with their mouths almost touching, 'He's been there, my own, lying in wait, ready to spring out and get you—like this,' his mouth collided with hers, 'and this,' he rolled her over and spread across her, 'and he's going to make love—and, my darling, I do mean love—to you as he's never done before.'

She felt him making short work of removing all of her barriers to their closeness, followed by his own. 'Please, Evan, please explain.' He was too busy lighting fires all over her pliant body to do so. He lifted himself above her and found the torch, playing it over her milky whiteness, then on to her rapturous face. 'Tell me, Evan, tell me before we——'

'What shall I tell you?' He pretended to consider. 'That I love you back?'

His mouth settled over one pink-tipped breast, then moved to the other. His hand ran over her stomach and found intimate places, making her arch and writhe and reach out her arms towards him. 'That I've wanted you,' he went on huskily, 'from the moment I saw you at the chalet and fell in love with you about two minutes later? That I couldn't resist, even if I'd wanted to, that warm-hearted young woman who tried so bravely to ski on her own, then ran into my arms and wrapped herself around me and that that was when I became doubly determined to marry her? Because it's all true, every word of it. It's all true.'

'But why,' she asked, when she could find sufficient breath, 'did you pretend to be indifferent and say you agreed to a non-emotional relationship?'

'I'd been through it all before, Francesca.' His voice lingered over her name in the way she loved. 'A man gets wary—it's the instinct to survive in today's kind of love jungle that makes him so. The disillusionment is painful and lasting. And you'd told me your position, too, remember. We both of us were willing to take a chance—that much was obvious—but a calculated chance.'

'So marriage without total commitment was your way of avoiding getting hurt a second time?'

He lifted a shoulder. 'It was no guarantee, but I was only too willing to try it—with you. It was also my way of going carefully with you. I wanted to marry you—no question about that—and the last thing I wanted to do was frighten you away.'

'Softly, softly?' she queried, running her fingers around his jaw.

'Very softly,' was his reply as his hand skimmed around her curving shape. 'Now——'

'Wait,' she pleaded, 'Just a few more moments.' He gave an indulgent, long-suffering sigh. 'Why did you keep warning me off Ralph?'

'Why? I'm fond of my stepbrother and knew that not under any circumstances was he going to get you, his girlfriend, back. If he got too deeply involved with the woman I intended to marry, he'd get badly hurt and I couldn't allow that. Plus, I have to admit it,' he nuzzled her throat and she shivered with pleasure, 'a generous helping of jealousy.'

Fran nodded. 'Just one more thing. That day on the 'phone when you spoke to me in German, what did you say?'

A chuckle rumbled low in his chest. 'I said, *Hast du was besonders, heut abend, vor Ich will mit dir schlafen.* Which roughly means, Have you anything special planned for tonight because I want to sleep with you! In other words, are you doing anything tonight because I want to make love to you. Okay?' He pinched her chin.

'If only I'd known!' she cried. 'I'd have said yes, please, and we'd have been saved so much unhappiness.'

'True,' he agreed, 'but it's behind us now.' He shifted and tightened his hold. 'We've talked too long,' he said gruffly. 'Now the ice between us has gone, let the fire between us burn.'

'Love me, Evan,' she urged, straining towards him, 'really love me.'

'Just try and stop me,' he growled. 'For the first time, my darling—and there'll be many more—we'll make love *with love*. With all our feelings and all our hearts.'

And they did.

When dawn came a long time later, it looked into the tiny window and found them asleep in each other's arms.

Harlequin Presents

Coming Next Month

Available in June wherever paperback books are sold, or through Harlequin Reader Service.

In the U.S.
901 Fuhrmann Blvd.
P.O. Box 1397
Buffalo, N.Y. 14240-1397

In Canada
P.O. Box 2800, Postal Station A
5170 Yonge Street
Willowdale, Ontario M2N 6J3

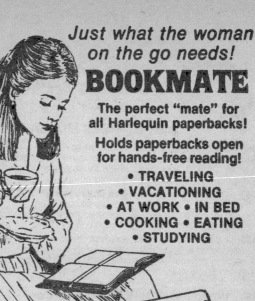
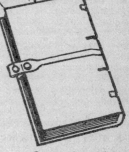

Can you keep a secret?

You can keep this one plus 4 free novels

WORLDWIDE LIBRARY IS YOUR TICKET TO ROMANCE, ADVENTURE AND EXCITEMENT

Experience it all in these big, bold Bestsellers— Yours exclusively from WORLDWIDE LIBRARY WHILE QUANTITIES LAST

To receive these Bestsellers, complete the order form, detach and send together with your check or money order (include 75¢ postage and handling), payable to WORLDWIDE LIBRARY, to:

In the U.S.

WORLDWIDE LIBRARY
901 Fuhrmann Blvd.
Buffalo, N.Y. 14269

In Canada

WORLDWIDE LIBRARY
P.O. Box 2800, 5170 Yonge Street
Postal Station A, Willowdale, Ontario
M2N 6J3

Quant.	Title	Price
_____	**WILD CONCERTO**, Anne Mather	$2.95
_____	**A VIOLATION**, Charlotte Lamb	$3.50
_____	**SECRETS**, Sheila Holland	$3.50
_____	**SWEET MEMORIES**, LaVyrle Spencer	$3.50
_____	**FLORA**, Anne Weale	$3.50
_____	**SUMMER'S AWAKENING**, Anne Weale	$3.50
_____	**FINGER PRINTS**, Barbara Delinsky	$3.50
_____	**DREAMWEAVER**, Felicia Gallant/Rebecca Flanders	$3.50
_____	**EYE OF THE STORM**, Maura Seger	$3.50
_____	**HIDDEN IN THE FLAME**, Anne Mather	$3.50
_____	**ECHO OF THUNDER**, Maura Seger	$3.95
_____	**DREAM OF DARKNESS**, Jocelyn Haley	$3.95

YOUR ORDER TOTAL	$_____
New York and Arizona residents add appropriate sales tax	$_____
Postage and Handling	$___.75
I enclose	$_____

NAME _____

ADDRESS _____ APT.# _____

CITY _____

STATE/PROV. _____ ZIP/POSTAL CODE _____

WW-1-3